MW00881847

DOOMSDAY DANI

CARISSA TURPIN

DOOMSDAY DANI

Maitland, Florida

© 2022 Carissa Turpin

All rights reserved. No part of this book may be transmitted in any form or by any means, electronic or mechanical, including photocopying, recording, or by any information storage or retrieval system, in part, in any form, without the permission of the publisher.

Orange Blossom Publishing
Maitland, Florida
www.orangeblossombooks.com
info@orangeblossombooks.com

First Edition: March 2023

Library of Congress Control Number: 2022922411

Edited by: Arielle Haughee
Formatted by: Autumn Skye
Cover design: Sanja Mosic

Print ISBN: 978-1-949935-64-6
eBook ISBN: 978-1-949935-65-3

Printed in the U.S.A.

Dedication

To the three most important people in my life: Mom, Dad, and Courtney. Thank you for helping me survive Y2K and a number of catastrophes since.

Table of Contents

Y2K: Noun. Abbreviation for the year 2000. Used to refer to the problems that were expected with computers when the date changed from 1999 to 2000.

Example: Many industry experts today believe the Y2K problem was exaggerated.

Source: The Cambridge English Dictionary

Worried About Y2K? Start Here.

By: Professor Prepared (professorprepared.com)

Hello, fellow preppers. You've likely stumbled upon this website due to your concerns about Y2K, also known as the Y2K Bug, Millennium Glitch, or Year 2000 Problem. Please know that no matter what your relatives, neighbors, or the news media might tell you, Y2K is a frightening possibility. You are right to look for ways to prepare yourself and your family.

To truly understand what you might need in the weeks and months following the Y2K disaster, it's important to understand what the Y2K bug is and how it will impact your community. I am writing this on February 22nd, 1999, and, as of this writing, everything in our world runs via computer. Our banks, power plants and nuclear facilities, food production plants, and telephones and communication systems are all heavily managed via computer.

It's our reliance on computers, however, that might lead to our downfall. In the vast majority of computing systems, the year is represented by a two-digit number. For example, my computer reads today's date as 2/22/99. At the stroke of midnight on January 1st, 2000, that number will become "00," making it completely indistinguishable from the year 1900 in our computer's electronic brain. This confusion can—and likely will—lead to errors of all sorts on an alarming scale.

Imagine—you will be plunged into darkness as electricity fails. You won't be able to withdraw your hard earned money from computerized ATMs. Phones will cut off, making communication with emergency medical services impossible. And, most frighteningly, the facilities where our nation's deadliest weapons are stored will scramble to contain them.

It's a scary (and likely) possibility, but you've taken the first step by visiting my website. Here, you will find information about storing food, cash, and medical supplies. You will find information about keeping your family safe and together should you need to "bug out" and leave your home for another location. There is also information about basic first aid, water purification, and talking to your friends and family about the upcoming disaster. All I ask in return is that you share this information with others—and, if you feel so inclined, you may mail a check or money order to the P.O. box below.

Stay safe, stay informed, and prepare for the worst. Good luck to you.

Click this link to visit the Professor Prepared Store! There you will find fully-stocked bug out bags, Professor Prepared merchandise, and more! We accept all major credit cards.

Chapter One

December 16th, 1999

15 Days Before

The world is ending soon, and we can be prepared; I know it. But all Mom can think about is Christmas cookies.

We're in the kitchen. The cookies have cooled on the stovetop, and Mom is allowing Shelby to scoop spoonfuls of red and green icing on their browned tops. Shelby is excited; she's bobbing up and down and poking her tongue through a hole where one of her front teeth should be. Mom seems happy, too, which is sort of a relief, because a few days ago I overheard her crying in the shower. She's smiling now, though, and she has on her favorite apron—it has an embroidered goose wearing a chef's hat. I'm happy they're having fun. There might not be much time for fun left.

Which is why I wish they would listen to me.

"You can store flour a really long time," I tell her. "Maybe you shouldn't waste it on cookies. Or store what you have leftover. You can put it on one of the shelves in my room." I gesture behind me, toward my bedroom, even though Mom obviously knows where it is.

1

Mom kisses Shelby's tiny head, right on the part of her hair. Then she straightens and glares at me. There's a string of Christmas lights wrapped around the light fixture above the kitchen table, and they make Mom's head glow like an angel. She'd never allow us to decorate the kitchen normally. Maybe she doesn't think we have much time left, either. But I don't think that's the reason.

"Dani," she hisses. "You're scaring your little sister. Can you knock it off with that doomsday talk for one night?"

I look at Shelby. She doesn't look scared. She's humming *Jingle Bells* under her breath and prying open a container of Christmas tree sprinkles. Normally, she'd never be allowed to decorate. *Too messy*, Mom always said.

"I'm trying to help," I say. "Professor Prepared said sharing knowledge is the key to—-"

Mom sighs and throws up her hands. She wrenches open one of the cabinets, pulls out a plate, and plops two sloppy cookies onto it. She shoves the plate at me.

"If you're going to talk like that, go somewhere else," she says. "Go to your room and eat. Please. I can't handle this gloomy stuff every day. It's nearly Christmas."

"It's nearly *Christmas*," Shelby parrots, slinging a generous amount of sprinkles onto a cookie.

I obey her, but I stomp my feet all the way to my bedroom.

I don't like being banished to my room, but I have to admit, it's the place where I feel safest.

I have a faded blue bedspread (Mom keeps saying we need to get a new one, and I refuse—what's the point of a bedspread, anyway?) and a poster of a black Volkswagen Beetle on one wall. I've put a few pencil sketches up with masking tape—mostly characters from my favorite video game, *Bounty Crescent*, but I also have a sketch of Shelby sleeping on the living room sofa and one of my own hand holding a pencil. I also have a small vanity mirror and bench. Mom insisted I'd get a lot of use out of the mirror as I "grew into a young lady," but, so far, I haven't spent any time staring at myself. There's no need—I know what I look like. I'm short, like Mom, and freckled like Dad. I have Mom's white-blonde hair and Dad's green eyes. All I usually wear are plaid button downs over t-shirts. Sometimes I'll even go for a sweatshirt with a handy kangaroo pocket, something that drives Mom crazy as we live in sweltering Phoenix. But makeup and fashion, as I tell Mom, are not survival skills.

The most exciting part of my room is my computer. It's technically the family's computer, but I use it the most. It sits on a black wooden desk. There's also a desk chair with wheels, and there's a weird squiggle on the cushion that Shelby made with a permanent marker. The monitor is a hard, white plastic shell. The computer is usually pretty noisy—sometimes it makes grinding sounds or whirring sounds, and when I log onto the internet, it screeches like a mad cat. Dad knows everything about computers, so he would probably be able to explain what the computer is doing at all times. I've never bothered to ask him, though, and now it doesn't really matter. The monitor is on, showing my newest desktop wallpaper—the mustached avatar of Professor Prepared. In the corner of the screen, I notice my instant messenger has gone idle.

I spend a lot of time on the computer, but it isn't my favorite part of my room. That would be the two sturdy steel shelves stocked with essentials—my newest addition. The shelves once stood in our garage and held normal things like jumper cables and tool boxes and extra light bulbs. But when Dad moved out, he told me I could have them. He gave me a funny look when I told him what I wanted to use them for, but when I reminded him of the time he bought a glass curio cabinet to store his *Star Wars* figurines, he didn't really say anything else. There are now neat rows of canned goods (some I swiped from the pantry, but most I bought with my allowance), two plastic jugs of drinking water, a glass jar containing a pocket knife, a small screwdriver, match sticks, and batteries, and a plastic tarp folded into a small square. It's not much—maybe only enough to last our family three weeks or so after Y2K. But it will buy us some time while we figure out what to do next.

Whenever Mom comes into my room and sees my shelves, she huffs. Shelby always tries to mess up the organization system of my cans. Professor Prepared says skepticism is normal, so I try not to take it personally. They'll be thankful for my prepping on January 1st, and that's what's important.

I plop onto my bed, settling the plate of cookies on my lap. After scarfing down the first cookie, I reach for my Game Grasp on the bedside table. I switch it on, letting the beeps of *Bounty Crescent* soothe me. A boy in my

Art class told me that *Bounty Crescent* was the most boring video game ever made. He told me I should play "real video games" and then listed a bunch of titles where the main character shoots bad guys with a machine gun or, even stupider, a gorilla goes around an island collecting bananas. I'm not interested in those at all. I don't think *Bounty Crescent* is boring; in fact, most of the time, I feel like it was made for me. In the game, I am overseeing a large farm. I've got to water and harvest my crops, feed my animals, and create positive relationships with the townspeople. Sometimes, when I feel nervous or sad, disappearing into *Bounty Crescent* and putting my tomato plants into neat rows makes me feel a whole lot better.

I'm brushing my newly milked cow when I hear a different sort of beeping. My instant messenger is flashing green on the monitor of my computer. I chew and swallow my final cookie and switch off my Game Grasp.

Last year, when my friend Natalie transferred to a different middle school, I downloaded instant messenger so we could stay in contact. We talked nearly every day. Then I sent her some links about Y2K and Professor Prepared. Since then, she only answers my messages every other week or so, and never chats for very long. I'm trying not to take it personally. Thinking about Natalie always makes my stomach hurt, though.

There are only three more "friends" on my instant messenger. One is Dad, but he's never on, even though he told me I could message him whenever I needed to talk during the week. The second is Trinity, but, despite the fact that we've been in the same classes since kindergarten, she's not my friend. In fact, she's the exact opposite of a friend. We got paired up for a project in Journalism, though, and we needed to talk to one another. Communicating through messenger seemed less painful than going to her house or talking to her on the phone. I should have deleted her after we turned everything in, but she's still there. Her status is away; she's posted some stupid song lyric about butterflies. I roll my eyes.

My third "friend" is Riley, and he's the one who's messaged me. He's my actual friend, I guess, even though he only moved here a few months ago. Things like friends and enemies don't really matter anymore. Professor Prepared says that *petty squabbles and weak friendships disappear in moments of catastrophe*. I click on Riley's name, opening a smaller chat screen.

Hey, he says.

A second later, he asks, *doing anything fun this weekend?*

I place my fingers on the keyboard, prepared to tell him all about how I'm going to my Dad's to celebrate Christmas. How it's boring and a little sad, and how Shelby and I have to share one creaky mattress. How it will be the first time it won't be the four of us—Mom, Dad, Shelby, and me—opening gifts and drinking hot cocoa and wading through a bunch of ripped wrapping paper.

I realize, though, that when I tell him this, I'll sound sad. And I don't want to sound sad, because being sad doesn't matter. I don't have time to be sad. I'm only prepared.

So, I decide to ignore Riley's message. I log off instant messenger, and it makes a noise like a slamming door. Then I shut down my computer and go back to brushing my cow.

Chapter Two

December 17th, 1999

14 Days Before

In Journalism class, Mr. Dennis reminds us it is the last day of school before winter break. I think about raising my hand to tell him it is the last day of school forever, but I decide against it.

"You need to make a lot of progress on your 'Me in the New Millennium' project," he says, clapping his hairy hands together. "Remember, you're focusing on who you are and who you want to be. Think about your interests, your friends, your extracurriculars. Turn it into a video, and I'll choose one outstanding submission to air on the morning news."

Out of the corner of my eye, I see Trinity smile and flip a strand of red hair over her shoulder. She's wearing those stupid butterfly clips with springs beneath the wings, so it looks like the butterflies' wings are flapping with every movement of her head. Ridiculous.

"The project is due January 7th," Mr. Dennis says, and then turns to write the date on the board as though we didn't hear him. He underlines it. "I'll give you the class period to work. Let me know if you need my help. Now scatter."

That's our signal to get out of our desks and head into the back of the classroom, where the newsroom is. There are quite a few elective classes at Lowell Middle School, but Journalism is by far the best. The space is bigger, and there are a few heavy video cameras on tripods. We have a wooden "news desk" with a panther, our school mascot, painted on the front. On another wall, we used butcher paper to create a blue background with a sun and a cloud. I painted a smile on the sun and a frown on the cloud, and whoever is in charge of reading the weather for the morning news show stands in front of it. There's always clutter—sometimes there will be basketballs or baseballs for sports segments or costumes if Mr. Dennis gives permission to film something silly. Last week, one of my classmates dressed up as a banana and did a rap about the school's salad bar.

I walk over to the news desk. There are papers on top of it, so I shuffle them and try to look busy so Mr. Dennis won't notice I'm not doing anything.

"Hey," someone says. "Did you get my message?"

It's Riley. He's smiling, and his hands are jammed into the pockets of his jeans. He wears the same shirt—a print of a football helmet and a football—every day, but in a variety of colors. I once asked him if he liked sports. He said he hated sports, but he liked not wasting time deciding on a shirt when he got ready for school in the morning. When he explained it like that, I actually thought it was a pretty smart idea.

What Riley really *does* love is zombies. He always carries around a book from the *Zombies of the Saguaro Desert* book series, and there's always a half-rotten face on the cover. I once made the mistake of asking him about the books, and he talked my ear off until the bell rang.

"I didn't get your message," I lie. I can't look him in the eye when I say it. Lying to Riley reminds me of the times I tell Shelby that her drawings are great when, in reality, they just look like crayon scribbles.

"Oh," Riley says. He drums his knuckles on the edge of the news desk. "I was just saying hey. Are you finished with your project?"

"I'm not doing it," I say. I try to keep my voice quiet so only Riley hears.

"Why?" Riley asks. "I can man the video camera, if you need—"

"There's no point," I say. "We won't be back after winter break, you know."

Riley nods. "Right. The Y2K thing."

"It's not a *thing*," I say, and my voice is louder than it normally is, especially with Riley. I gaze back down at the stack of papers, take a deep breath, and lower it. "Professor Prepared says that with every passing day, it's clear that big companies aren't taking this seriously, and we're heading for disaster."

"Oh yeah, Professor Prepared," Riley says. He scratches the back of his head, and his dark bangs fall into his eyes. "I read all that stuff you sent me."

My mouth drops open. No one reads the stuff I send them about Y2K and Professor Prepared. "Really? What did you think?"

Riley takes a deep breath, but whatever he's about to say is cut short. Trinity plops behind the news desk. She finagled her way into lead anchor, so she sits behind the desk every day when the cameras are rolling. She kicks her feet up, comfortable, and smiles, showing off her purple braces.

"I need someone to film me doing a back handspring. Mr. Dennis said it was fine if I did one in here, as long as I was safe. Can I borrow you, Riley?" She looks between the two of us, those idiotic butterflies bouncing on top of her head.

"Sure. What's a back handspring?" Riley asks.

"It's a really advanced flip," Trinity says. "I'm pretty much the only girl in my gymnastics class who can do one and get my hands in the right spot. That's what my 'Me in the Millennium' project is going to be about— gymnastics. I don't know where I would be without it. My coach says I might be able to compete at the national level someday."

I once read on Professor Prepared that being physically flexible and agile is actually pretty useful, but I can't let Trinity know that. Instead, I make some sort of noise, between a laugh and a scoff. Trinity's gaze drifts to me.

"What's your project about, Danielle? The apocalypse?"

Something about the way she always uses my full name has my hands clenched into fists. *Danielle* has never felt right to me. It feels more like a name for a girl who wears butterfly clips and has more than one friend who is really not that close of a friend at all. "Actually, I'm not doing the project. You guys shouldn't either. It's a waste of time."

Trinity laughs and spins a little in her desk chair. "I remember you talking about all that end-of-the-world stuff in PE before Mr. Morris told you to shut up. My dad says the people worried about Y2K are a bunch of conspiracy theorists and zealots. Zealot means that you're a radical—like really out there."

"I know what zealot means," I say, my voice a growl.

"He told me that people who freak out about that sort of stuff are out of touch with reality," Trinity continues, as though I didn't speak. "You're not out of touch with reality. Are you, Danielle?"

"No," I say. I look over at Riley, who is very focused on twisting the end of his shirt into a knot.

Trinity notices. "Riley, you're new to Lowell, so you might not know this. I'll fill you in, though. Danielle is a really gloomy person. She's not much fun to be around." She sticks her lip out in a pout and traces an imaginary tear down her cheek.

I am fully prepared to tell Trinity she should do a fancy back handspring off a very steep cliff when Mr. Dennis calls my name. He heads over to our group and hands me a paper hall pass.

"I just got off the phone with Ms. Paige," he says. "She says she needs to speak with you right away."

Ms. Paige is the guidance counselor, and her office is the exact opposite of my bedroom.

I've been in there a lot since I started middle school, so I know—the woman is obsessed with smiley faces. She has smiley face posters, two smiley face bean bags, and a smiley face coffee mug that holds her smiley face ink pens. And when I crack open her office door, she sees me and turns into a human smiley face.

"Dani Collier," she says, still smiling. "Have a seat, sweetheart."

I decide to sit in an ordinary chair instead of the bean bag.

Ms. Paige sighs, then leans back a bit in her desk chair. "Well, Dani, I just got a visit from Mrs. Michaels."

I roll my eyes. Mrs. Michaels is my English teacher, and she's extremely uptight. We once read a story with the word *darn* in it, and she refused to say it. She just skipped right over it, like it didn't exist.

"I know, I know," Ms. Paige says. She reaches into one of her desk drawers and produces my black-and-white composition notebook, the one Mrs. Michaels requires us to journal in at the start of every class. She lays it on the desk between us.

"Mrs. Michaels is worried about you. She says your journal entries for the last week or so haven't been about the prompts she's written on the board," Ms. Paige says. "She said you're writing about Y2K. So, I flipped through it, and she's right."

"People should be able to journal about whatever they want," I say, but my head is hanging down, so I say it more to the ground than to Ms. Paige.

"Maybe," says Ms. Paige. "I think it's more about the content. It's dark, and that bothers her. She says she doesn't think it's appropriate for a twelve-year-old girl to dwell on this to such a degree." Ms. Paige tries to look serious, then she smiles a little. "What do you think about that?"

"You know what I think about that," I say.

Teachers have always been worried about me. They say my writing is too dark, or I'm too interested in "morbid" things. I was first called into Ms. Paige's office after I wrote an eleven-page paper on Typhoid Mary for World History class. During that visit, Ms. Paige told me that when she was my age, she was obsessed with natural disasters. Hurricanes, tornadoes, tsunamis, she loved them all and bored her parents to death with facts about avalanches and volcanic eruptions. It made me feel a lot better. Sometimes I'm called to Ms. Paige's office because another teacher is "concerned" about me, but sometimes she just calls me down to talk. She says I remind her of herself when she was a kid. *Kindred spirits*, she says. And I try not to let it show, but I like it when she says that.

"You know I think there's absolutely nothing wrong with being different," Ms. Paige says. "I think it's wonderful, actually. But what's concerning to me is the idea you might be very anxious about December 31st. And if you're worried, that could affect a lot of stuff, like school. How often do you worry about Y2K, Dani?"

I roll my eyes again. Professor Prepared says that uninformed people often mistake Y2K preparedness as being afraid. They think their confidence that nothing will happen is a sort of bravery.

"I don't worry about it," I say. "I'm ready for it. I think it's everyone else who should start worrying about it."

Ms. Paige tilts her head and studies me. "If you say you're not worried, I believe you. But I'm going to tell you something, and maybe if you're a little worried, somewhere deep down, it might make you feel better."

"I'm not worried," I repeat.

"My brother takes care of the technology at a big bank. He's the computer guy. And he told me they're absolutely prepared. They have protocols on top of protocols. If something goes wrong, they have a Plan B and a Plan C and so on and so on. He says all the banks' locations in other parts of the country have done the exact same thing."

"That's good," I say. "But there's more stuff to worry about than your brother's bank."

"But you're not worried?" Ms. Paige says with a grin.

"I'm not," I say. I look her in the eye, because it is one hundred percent true.

"Is there anything else you might be worried about? Anything going on at home?"

My throat suddenly feels tight and sore, like there's not enough room for my tonsils. "No."

Ms. Paige frowns and doesn't look convinced. "All right. Well, if you ask me, we are absolutely going to see each other again in the year 2000, Dani." Her smile returns, then she reaches over and squeezes my hand. I let her, even though it feels awkward. "Have a wonderful break," she says.

"You too," I say, standing. She smiles at me until I am able to softly shut her office door, blocking her from view.

Ms. Paige is super weird, I think, *but she's nice, and I hope she'll be okay.* I almost open the door again, to ask her if she has canned goods and bottled water, but I stop myself.

Journalism is the last class of the day, and by the time I leave Ms. Paige's office, there are only minutes left before the final bell rings. I walk extra slow to my locker, and as I do, I try to take in Lowell Middle School one last time. The closed doors of classrooms, their beginning-of-the-year decorations starting to peel and fall off. The flyers asking students to buy holiday candy grams to support the Pep Club. Finally, the rows of blue lockers, some of them dented, some of them rusting at the corners. *I've never loved school*, I think as I twirl my combination lock, *but I'll miss this place.*

The bell sounds, and a kid rushes past me, nearly knocking me over. Others follow—laughing and talking, excited to be done with school for the next three weeks. I want to scream at them to pay attention. *There's danger ahead! You're actually done with school forever! You should look at this place one last time, too.* But these words don't come out— they bubble up but stay put, like soapy suds in a sink.

I yank out my backpack and look across the hall to see Riley at his locker. He's putting his textbooks inside, still clutching a zombie book in the crook of his arm. He looks up, sees me, and waves.

I wave back.

He opens his mouth as though he wants to tell me something, but I sling on my backpack and walk as fast as I can to parent pickup. Dad's already there, in his station wagon. He's looking down at his lap, probably at his beeper. Shelby is in the back seat, her face pressed against the window. She pulls back and laughs at the smudge she made with her nose.

I groan and walk toward my weekend.

*What it Means to "Bug Out" and
Why You Should Prepare for It*

By: Professor Prepared (professorprepared.com)

*If you've visited this section of the website, it's clear you're
interested in the concept of "bugging out" after the highly likely
Y2K disaster. This is a term you've probably seen in spy novels or
heard in disaster movies. But what does it mean?*

*In the case of an event as crippling and widespread as Y2K,
resources like food, water, and gasoline will dwindle quickly. Looters
will first start with easy targets—they'll break into grocery and
department stores and hoard necessities. When all the retail locations have been thoroughly ransacked, they will then turn to neigh-
borhoods. These looters will stop at nothing to take essential items
from your household, including injuring you and your family.*

*It is also possible that computer malfunctions during Y2K
could contribute to the accidental release of chemical or biological
weapons. In this scenario, it would be imperative for you and your
family to leave your home in order to ensure your survival.*

*So, in short, to "bug out" means to leave your home or residence
in pursuit of a second, safer location. If you have a vacation home
or know of a secluded spot, you might think you have bugging out
covered, right?*

Wrong.

*Traveling from one location to another during the Y2K disaster
will be extremely perilous. Time will be of the essence. While
traveling by yourself or with a partner is easiest, traveling with a
family is still possible if every member of that family is well-pre-
pared. Here are some bug out basics everyone should practice, but
especially if you have a family larger than two:*

1. ***Make sure everyone knows to meet at a secure location***. *It's wisest to choose a spot outdoors, preferably in your yard or nearby. Make sure every member of the family knows to head to this particular spot in the event of an emergency.*

2. ***Practice packing essential items into your vehicle***. *All of the food and water you've stored and prepped will need to travel with you, but packing these items can waste precious time. Practice grabbing these items and getting them organized in your vehicle of choice. Have another family member time you, if possible.*

3. ***Plan for younger children***. *Younger children will not have the stamina or patience to endure a long journey. Make sure to bring simple, quiet toys to keep them occupied. It might be wise to purchase a wagon, sled, or stroller to transport young children if you need to travel by foot.*

Above all, it is important to stay calm and practice, practice, practice! While the world continues to panic and scramble as we inch closer to December 31st, I hope your preparedness has brought you some degree of comfort.

Stay safe, stay informed, and prepare for the worst. Good luck to you.

Still looking for supplies? Don't wait until the last minute. Click here to visit the Professor Prepared Store!

Chapter Three

December 18th, 1999

13 Days Before

When I think about Dad's apartment, I think about paper plates.

At home, we have all sorts of *real* plates. White porcelain plates with black rings around the edges, plastic plates with cartoon characters or smiling animals. There's even a plate I made at day camp when I was six with my tiny handprints frozen in the middle.

But Dad's plates are always paper. And his cups and utensils are disposable, too. It makes me feel like I'm at a picnic or cookout, not the place where my dad lives. The rest of the apartment isn't much better. His fridge smells like cleaner and only has bottles of water and beer. There are only a few microwaveable meals in the freezer. The chairs and small table in the living room are part of a patio set we once had on the back deck at home. His TV is nice, but it sits on a large box of unpacked clothes. I guess that's good, though. The less stuff he has, the easier it will be for him to leave it all behind on New Year's Eve.

I'm sitting in one of the hard, springy chairs, eating my second piece of pizza from a paper plate. Dad and Shelby are sitting on the floor. Dad bought some sort of game for us to play—the box contained a green plastic crocodile with two rows of removable teeth. He explained that with a pair of toy pliers, you are supposed to remove a tooth from the crocodile's smiling mouth, then pass the pliers to another player. But if the crocodile chomps its mouth shut while you're trying to pull its tooth, you're out. Shelby was instantly excited; I told him I'd just watch.

Shelby shrieks with glee as the motorized crocodile gently shuts its mouth over her tiny fingers.

"You're out!" Dad says. He's smiling, and the light from the TV is reflecting off his glasses.

"Nuh uh," Shelby says, hugging her arms around herself. "I'll try again. Okay?"

"Okay," Dad says, sighing as if he's annoyed. He's not, though. He's smiling. Shelby has asked for a do-over at least three times. He quickly sticks the teeth back in the crocodile's mouth, and Shelby raises the pliers again.

"Dad," I say.

"You want to play, Dani?" he asks. "You can take my spot, if you want. I think I'm too old to sit on the floor." He winces and rubs his back.

"No, that's not it," I say. I take one last bite of pizza crust. "You're still planning to come over on the 31st, right?"

Dad's face wrinkles in confusion for a moment. I'm nervous, so I focus on chewing and swallowing. Finally,

Dad shrugs. "I hope so. I might have to go in and monitor the computers at work—"

Shelby screeches as the crocodile bites her again.

"We need to be together," I say. I'm trying to stay calm, but I feel my stomach swooping with anger. It's a feeling I hate—like missing a step on a staircase and waiting to hit the ground. "I told you it was important, and you said you'd be there."

"I'll try again," Shelby says, and starts putting the crocodile teeth back in herself.

"I am hoping to be there," Dad says. "Really, Dani. But I have to make sure everything rolls over correctly at work."

"It's not going to," I say. "Professor Prepared says we can't waste time being hopeful. We have to face the most likely outcome."

"Dani," Dad says. He's using his "warning" voice. The one he uses when I'm talking back or not doing my homework, and I'm one step away from being grounded.

"Just try, okay? Remember—we're meeting at the cactus beside the driveway at midnight. Mom, Shelby, and I have practiced, but since you haven't been there—"

"I can remember," Dad says, and by the tone of his voice and the frown on his face, I know that now he *is* actually annoyed, and not the fun fake annoyed he was with Shelby.

On the floor, the crocodile has chomped Shelby's fingers, but she doesn't react. She is instead half slumped over, her eyes drooping, her head wobbling.

"I think it's time for bed," Dad says, gently pulling her hand free. "Santa is coming early. I called him up."

Shelby's eyes pop open. "You called the North Pole?"

Dad nods as though it's no big deal. "I told him you two would be here this weekend. He said he'll be here in the morning, so we've got to be well-rested."

Shelby looks at me, her mouth hanging open as though Dad is spilling a bunch of government secrets. "Okay," she says, and races toward our bedroom.

I can actually tell that Dad tried to make mine and Shelby's room a nice place. We only have a mattress, no bed frame yet, but Dad put on a pink bedsheet and bought floral pillows. The only other things in the room are Dad's technology magazines. They're in three large stacks in the far corner. Mom always said they were useless, and Dad was a hoarder; Dad argued that he needed them to stay up-to-date at his job. It was one of the things they fought about at the end.

Shelby bounces over to her side of the bed and buries her face in one of the pillows. I stop myself from doing the same, even though the pillow case feels cool against my skin. Dad bends and kisses the top of Shelby's head. He reaches over and pats one of my hands. "Goodnight, girls," he says.

Shelby tells him goodnight. I'm lying on top of the bedsheet and thinking about earlier, so I don't respond. I'm too busy imagining my new worst fear—Mom, Shelby, and me standing around the big cactus without Dad.

Dad turns off the light and shuts the door. I turn away, staring toward the shapes of the magazine stacks in the dark.

Whenever Shelby and I stay the night with Dad, I always wonder what Mom is doing. If she's asleep, if she's up baking a cake or a loaf of banana bread to take her mind off her empty house. Mom always likes to bake when she feels anxious, and in the last year or so, she's baked *a lot*. When I'm home, I think of Dad—whether or not he misses having normal plates, if he's reading all his magazines in peace without Mom's nagging and me and Shelby interrupting him. It makes my brain tired to constantly think about one parent or the other. *At least on January 1st, everyone will be in one place*, I think.

I can't remember when I noticed Mom and Dad weren't getting along. I could hear them, sometimes, shouting through my bedroom wall long after I went to bed. Once, we drove to Tucson to visit the Air and Space Museum, and they got into an argument. The details are kind of fuzzy, because I immediately closed my eyes and tried to stop listening, but it was something to do with Dad's work schedule. Mom said Dad was an "absentee father," and then Dad said Mom was a "control freak." After that, Mom refused to talk for the rest of the ride, staring straight ahead, not even responding to Shelby and me. And, in the weeks after our trip to Tucson, there were times when Dad wouldn't come home for dinner, and Mom would say he was working late. Sometimes, he didn't come home until the next day. Mom was especially quiet on those days. Dad even missed Shelby's preschool graduation because of work. Mom said it was okay and that she'd take pictures to show Dad, but I knew she was just pretending for Shelby and me. I sat next to her, and I didn't miss how her hand trembled the entire cere-mony, and how her eyes were glassy with tears when they handed Shelby her tiny diploma. When the pictures were developed, Shelby looked like a blur in a cap and gown.

On the Fourth of July, Mom, Dad, Shelby, and I went to the park to see the fireworks. We sat on a blanket and ate red, white, and blue popsicles. Mom lathered us in sunscreen and bug repellant and used the opportunity to kiss us both on the cheek. Dad and I played round after round of Rock, Paper, Scissors, only stopping when it grew dark and the fireworks began. We cheered at the finale, when the sky lit up with so many fireworks it was hard to tell them apart. I felt tired when it was all over, but the good kind of tired—the way you feel when you're a little kid and you play all day without taking a break. Then we rolled up the blanket and picked up our trash and headed to the parking lot. We got back in our minivan to head home, and as we sat in traffic, Dad looked at Shelby and me in the rearview mirror.

"Girls," he'd said. "Your Mom and I have something to tell you."

And he told us. He found an apartment; he would be moving in a matter of days. Shelby and I would stay in the house with Mom and visit him on the weekends. It didn't really change anything, Mom said. They both still loved us very much. She asked if we had any questions.

Shelby was too young to understand. She's only in kindergarten, so she's actually still too young to understand. I understood perfectly, but I only shook my head and stared out the window. There was nothing but the dark, smoky sky and the glow of the other cars' headlights. All I could think was that I wanted to jump out of the van and sit in someone else's car and be a part of someone else's family.

And Mom was wrong—everything changed. Dad was suddenly gone. He said we'd spend the weekend together, but every few weekends he'd have to cancel because he was needed at work. He'd call us instead, but talking to Dad on the phone was much different than having Dad around in person, giving Shelby piggyback rides and challenging me to a level of *Super Mario Brothers*.

Mom was different, too. Before, she'd been so strict about cleanliness and organization—Shelby and I were expected to tidy our room every week, and we were constantly told to keep our good school clothes clean. After Dad left, Mom let Shelby play with Play Doh on the carpet. She only laughed and found the scissors when Shelby got a wad of chewing gum stuck in her hair. When an ink pen exploded on one of my newer button ups, Mom only shrugged and told me we'd go shopping for a new one. This new Mom seemed like an imposter, which made me uncomfortable. I tried to stay in my room and play my Game Grasp and draw. I fantasized that one day Mom and Dad would admit that everything had just been one big practical joke and that our family could go back to normal.

Not long after Dad moved into his apartment, Shelby and I came for a visit. Dad and Shelby watched some kid movie on TV. I was bored, so I went to our room and sifted through Dad's magazines.

One of the pages immediately caught my eye. There was a picture at the top of a giant cartoon bug with three legs and a long antenna. It had red eyes, and on its blue back were three symbols: Y2K. It appeared to be crawling on top of a desktop computer. The screen on the monitor was blue, and a giant red X stretched from corner to corner.

The title of the article was printed in bold, black letters beneath the picture of the bug: "Are We Ready for Y2K?"

I was intrigued. Most of the articles in the magazines were about the best brand of printer or how to make money selling your stuff on eBay. So, I read on, and discovered, with horror, that the world was months away from total collapse, and no one had ever told me. I thought of my computer at home, in my bedroom. I imagined it swelling and getting bigger the closer we got to December 31st until it was ready to explode. I imagined bugs seeping through the cracks and lines of the monitor, spilling onto the keyboard, tumbling onto the floor of my bedroom. An absolute infestation.

One of the people quoted in the article was a man who went by the alias Professor Prepared. He wouldn't allow his photograph to appear in the magazine, but he did encourage readers to visit his website and online store. "Some may call me paranoid," he said. "But there's nothing more important to me than family. When the world turns to chaos, labels like *scaredy cat* or *neurotic* just won't matter. What will matter is that my family is together and safe, so I strive to be as prepared as possible. You can visit my online store and be as prepared as possible, too."

I can remember bursting back into the living room and showing the article to Dad.

"Don't worry about it, Dani," Dad said, a little loudly because Shelby was singing along with the movie. "People have known about Y2K for years. All the people I know who work in tech have been preparing for it."

"But not us," I said, pointing to a graphic in the article that listed the supplies to have on hand.

"We're fine," Dad said. "It's nothing you need to worry about."

I took the magazine home and read the article word-for-word to Mom.

"That sounds far-fetched," Mom said between icing cupcakes. "Like something out of a movie."

"But what will we do if it happens?" I asked.

"What we do best," Mom said, pausing to lick a stray blob of icing from her wrist. "Figure it out as we go."

I realized, then, that it would be up to me to prepare my family. After Y2K, I decided, Mom and Dad wouldn't have time to be angry, to argue. All that would matter was that we were all safe. And, most importantly, *together*.

Shelby's sniffling snaps me out of my thoughts. She lets out a choked little cry and snuggles closer to me.

"What's wrong?" I ask. I'm whispering, even though Dad's room is all the way on the other side of the apartment.

Shelby chokes out another cry. In the dark, I can barely see her hands come up to rub her eyes. "Dani," she says. "I'm scared."

Uh oh, I think. Mom was right after all. She's been listening to me talk about Y2K, and now I've freaked her out.

"Don't be scared," I say, and rub her back. "I'm on top of it. I have enough food and water for us to—"

"I *am* scared," Shelby repeats. "I don't think Daddy really called Santa on the phone. He was telling a fib. Santa doesn't know we're here. He won't know where we are, and we won't get our presents." After she says this, I feel her tiny shoulders shake as she starts to cry harder.

I know she can't see me, so I roll my eyes. I don't stop rubbing her back, though.

Chapter Four

December 19th, 1999

12 Days Before

I wake up when Shelby pokes me in the eye.

"Dani," she says. I feel one of her hands closing around my shoulder. "Santa found us! Daddy *did* call him! He came!" She shakes me. "Get up! Get up and see!"

I know she won't stop until I obey, so I groan and sit up. My back aches from sleeping on a mattress directly on the floor. I still feel angry, too, so there's still the twisty, uncomfortable feeling in my gut.

"Hurry up!" Shelby demands. I notice she's trembling a little, and bending one leg and then the other like she's in a marching band. Mom always says Ants-In-Her-Pants should have been Shelby's middle name.

I wobble to a standing position and head out to the living room. Dad didn't bother with a Christmas tree, so our presents are in a pile in the center of the space. Shelby hands me a bulging stocking.

"There's candy in there!" she squeals.

"Thanks for ruining the surprise," I grumble. I plop onto the floor, remembering at the last minute that Dad has downstairs neighbors.

But Dad doesn't say anything; he only laughs. He's sitting in one of the patio chairs, sipping coffee from a Styrofoam cup. He looks happy, and I suddenly feel like forgiving him for yesterday.

Shelby pulls item after item out of her stocking, barely looking at any of it. "Socks, a candy cane, a chocolate Santa...okay, time for presents!"

"We have to let Dani open her stocking first," Dad says.

Shelby groans and flops dramatically onto her back. Dad laughs again, and he and I share a secret smile. I pull out my own socks, candy cane, and chocolate Santa as slowly as possible. Shelby has practically rolled all over the floor by the time the stocking is empty.

"Okay, okay!" she yells. Her hair is now in fuzzy knots. "Time for presents!"

She doesn't waste any time and lunges forward, snatching a present from the pile. She can't really read yet, but she does know that her name starts with the letter S. She pauses only a second to check the nametag, then rips away the wrapping paper in one swipe. She gets a Barbie head mannequin with realistic hair to brush, a plastic shopping cart filled with plastic fruits and vegetables, a stuffed monkey wearing bright red lipstick, and a dollhouse with lights that go on and off. *Nice, quiet toys*, I think. *Everything except the dollhouse could travel with us. Although the lights in the dollhouse could come in handy if we needed to send a signal.* Shelby is still squealing over all her new gifts when Dad tells her she has one last present left.

Her tiny eyes frantically search the room, her hands bent like claws, ready to unwrap something else. "Where?" she asks.

Dad gets up and goes to his bedroom. He comes back seconds later pulling a bright red wagon with a big bow on top. My mouth drops open, and I leap to my feet. Shelby is jumping up and down and squealing—I can see her out of the corner of my eye—but my voice is louder.

"Dad," I say, jumping a little, too. "That's perfect!"

"You think so?" Dad asks. His smile looks wide and pleased, like the smile he uses when we have fun on vacation or laugh at a funny movie he picked out. "I didn't know if she'd be too old for it, but everyone needs a wagon to—"

"If we have to bug out on foot, we'll be able to put her in it," I say. "Professor Prepared said that younger children can't travel long distances. Now that we have one of these, we can take her anywhere!"

I expect Dad to be even happier, knowing his present has so many different uses. Instead, the smile falls off his face. He doesn't even laugh when Shelby climbs into the wagon and presses the big bow to the top of her head.

"I'm a present!" she laughs.

"Your turn, Dani," Dad says quietly.

Something in the room changes. Even Shelby feels it. She takes the bow off her head, then stands to grab her stuffed monkey. She climbs back into the wagon without another word.

I suddenly feel embarrassed, and I open my presents quietly, as though one false move would cause them to explode. I unwrap a sweatshirt that says *Phoenix* on it, but the *o* is replaced with a succulent, a blue and black lava lamp, and a long tube that holds a glossy *Bounty Crescent* poster. For one small moment, I feel giddy and warm, the way I feel when I see the *Bounty Crescent* loading screen.

"You still like that, right?" Dad says when I open it, but he is looking at the wall above my head instead of me. His stiffness makes me remember the tension in the room, and that makes me want to stop opening presents and go back to bed.

"Yeah, I love it," I say. And I do. My heart aches when I think about leaving the poster and my Game Grasp behind on the 31st.

My final gift is tucked inside a tiny box—a wad of cash. It's the only thing I really asked for. I take it out and put it in the pocket of my pajamas, feeling as though it would be rude to count it. In my mind, I know exactly where I'll stick it—the glass jar on one of the shelves in my bedroom. It's good to have a specific place to store cash, especially if the electricity goes out.

"Thank you," I say. My voice feels too loud. "The cash will really come in handy." I don't explain why it will come in handy. We both know.

Dad finally looks me in the eye. He holds his Styrofoam cup downward; there's no longer any coffee in it. He must have drunk it in several big gulps while I was opening my gifts. "Promise me something, Dani," he says.

"Okay," I say. Something about his voice makes my stomach swoop like it did last night and, in my mind, I'm missing a step all over again.

"Once all this Y2K stuff is over—"

I start to tell him it will never be over. Even after January 1st, Y2K will affect every aspect of our lives. But I think better of it.

"—please spend that money on something normal."

I blink, surprised. "Normal?"

Dad nods. "Get an MP3 player or one of those cordless phones you can see through or a Tamagotchi. Something kids your age have," he says. "Something normal."

"Normal," I repeat, just because I want to say the word myself. It feels bad and hateful coming out of my mouth.

I think of the rage I felt burning my face when Trinity called me a "gloomy person." I imagine Mrs. Michaels looking at my composition notebook, her eyes widening in alarm. And then I think of Dad's meticulous magazine stacks and the figurines he once kept behind glass.

Normal. Didn't Dad, of all people, know that was something I just couldn't be?

Dad is helping Shelby open all of her toys—the Barbie mannequin has small plastic hair brushes and fake hairspray that need to be unscrewed from the box; the dollhouse has stickers that need to be carefully placed in the correct rooms.

I see my opportunity. Dad's phone is in the tiny kitchen, attached to the wall. I punch in Mom's number, and it only rings once.

"Hello?" she sounds panicked.

"Mom, it's okay. It's me," I say. "Dani. Everything is okay." I'm wincing when I say it because my stomach still hurts. There's a pinching hurt between my eyes. Everything is not okay.

Mom lets out a long breath. "I saw your Dad's name on the caller ID and for some reason I just assumed the worst." She laughs a little into the phone, and it creates static. "You guys having a good Christmas with Dad? Did you get any good gifts?"

"Yeah," I say quickly. I crane my head to peer into the living room. Dad is still helping Shelby, who is twisting around impatiently. I keep remembering something. Once, in grade school, we took a field trip to a big cavern, and the tour guide yelled, *"Hello!"* when we had all hiked to the correct spot. His voice bounced off the rock walls until it sounded almost like a chorus. I can still hear the word *normal* echoing through my head as though Dad shouted it into a cavern.

"Can you come pick us up?" I finally ask.

Mom is quiet on the other end.

"I'm ready to come home," I add. I twirl the curly cord of the phone around my index finger.

"Are you safe?" Mom asks. "Is everything okay? What's wrong?"

"Nothing," I say. I know it sounds like a lie—I've never been a very good actress.

"You're supposed to be with your dad until this evening," Mom says.

"I know," I say. "And that's fine, really. But I miss you. And I left my Game Grasp there, so…"

"I don't think I should," Mom says.

"Please, Mom," I say.

"All right," she says. "I'll be there in fifteen minutes or so."

I go back into the living room. Dad has moved on to fiddling with the lights in Shelby's dollhouse. Something isn't working right; I hear him cursing under his breath. Shelby is stacking and restacking her plastic fruit and vegetables into the shopping cart. I sit and watch her, then pretend to nibble on the plastic food when she hands it to me. She giggles.

Minutes later, there's a knock at the door. Now my stomach feels like I've missed two steps. Maybe an entire flight.

Dad looks up, surprised, and murmurs something about Shelby and I staying put. "I'm not expecting anyone," he says. He looks through the peephole, grunts, then slips out the door.

I remain sitting next to Shelby on the carpet, but I strain my ears, listening closely. I hear the high pitch of Mom's voice, the gruffness of Dad's. Their conversation seems calm at first, and then I hear Dad say, "According to the custody agreement…" and Mom say "…old enough to make up her own mind." Then Dad says, "You know she's just going to look at that website all day, Sheila." Mom makes some sort of sound in response, almost like a chicken's cluck, and says, "Where do you think she learned about that website in the first place, Kenny?" It all makes me nervous. I want to go to the bathroom and hide, but that would mean leaving Shelby.

I look over at her, but she's oblivious, handing me a cluster of plastic grapes.

Dad says something else I can't make out, and then the front door opens again. He steps back in, and Mom is behind him.

Shelby gasps, "Mom!" and holds up a plastic can of creamed corn to show her.

The sequined Santa on Mom's shirt is smiling, but she isn't. Dad's cheeks are red, and there's a crease between his eyebrows.

He doesn't look at me, but he looks straight at Shelby. "Let's get these toys packed up," he says. "Your mom is here to get you."

Dealing with Naysayers

By: Professor Prepared (professorprepared.com)

Everyone copes with stress and trauma differently. As you prepare for the Y2K disaster, you will likely encounter friends, family members, or even strangers who do not believe the arrival of the new millennium poses any sort of threat. These people may dismiss your concerns or mock you outright. What should you do to change their minds?

First, direct them to this website. Show them the articles about food and water storage and home security. Explain what Y2K is and remind them how computer technology is integrated into almost every aspect of our daily lives. When presented with such compelling evidence, most reasonable people will soon see the light.

If they're still not convinced, share these true stories. Talk about **Theo Jacobs**, *a Harvard professor who has quit his job, sold his possessions, and moved "off the grid" in preparation for the Y2K disaster. Mention* **Sharon Pierce**, *a computer scientist who has been preparing her family for Y2K since the early 90s. Most people believe those who prepare for the Millennium Glitch are a small number of radical individuals when, in reality, most educated people now see the need for Y2K preparation.*

In the end, you cannot force others to see the world as you do. Although sharing information and resources is important, at the end of the day, all you can do is prepare yourself and your family. Keep your fingers crossed that naysayers you care about will soon change their minds before it's too late.

Stay safe, stay informed, and prepare for the worst. Good luck to you.

Want to convince your friends and neighbors to prepare for Y2K by showing off your impressive stash of survival gear? Visit the Professor Prepared Store!

Chapter Five

December 20th, 1999

11 Days Before

The next morning, I pour a huge bowl of Lucky Spangles and drown them in milk. I love cereal, especially cereal with sugary marshmallows, though it doesn't have the best shelf life. Milk is even more perishable. I don't have much longer to enjoy Lucky Spangles, so I try to eat them as often as I can.

I'm on my way back to my room to read Professor Prepared's latest blog entry when I nearly run into Mom in the hallway. She's carrying a hamper of dirty laundry, and she gestures at my bowl of cereal with her free hand.

"Eat fast," she says. "We're going to Nana and Pop's house."

I groan and lean against the wall, sounding a little like Shelby. "Really? Today?"

Mom raises an eyebrow. "Yes, today. Don't be rude. We'll need to leave in about twenty minutes."

Nana and Pop are Mom's parents. They're only in Phoenix half the year. After that, they stay in Tennessee with Mom's brother, because Pop hates the summer heat.

We don't see them often, but Mom always insists we go for a visit near Christmas. Their home is dark and cluttered and smells like the boxed-up clothes in our attic. They only watch black-and-white shows on television or the channel where adults are selling useless things like turquoise rings or fancy lotions. Sometimes they offer Shelby and me stale hard candy.

I seem to be the only person who doesn't want to visit Nana and Pop. Shelby is happy to go as long as she can take her Barbie head mannequin. We pile into the car, pull into the street, and I feel the uncomfortable quiet that comes before a big conversation. I reach for the volume on the radio, but Mom blocks my movements with her hand.

"So, are we going to talk about what happened at your dad's?" Mom asks. I'm sitting in the passenger's seat beside her; Shelby is humming to herself in the back.

"Nothing happened at Dad's," I say. I pretend to be interested in the landscape as we drive by—mostly palm trees and cacti wrapped in Christmas lights.

"Yet you wanted to come home eight hours early?" Mom asks, turning her head to look at me before concentrating on the road again.

"I told you, I missed you. And I wanted to play *Bounty Crescent*," I say.

Mom sighs, but doesn't press any further for the rest of the drive. That's new for her. When Dad was still around, she usually bothered me until I spit it out, then a conversation would follow about what I could do to resolve the situation. Mom used to always want to fix my problems, whether they were fixable or not. It really annoyed me at the time, and now I kind of miss it.

We pull up to Nana and Pop's house. They have a big lemon tree in their yard, and it makes it hard to see the front door. But Pop is waiting for us near the driveway, wearing suspenders over his big belly and leaning on his walking stick.

"Merry Christmas, Dad," Mom says. She kisses him on the cheek.

"Merry Christmas," Pop says. He leans down and kisses me on the cheek, then Shelby. His whiskers sting my face. Shelby must feel it too, because she giggles when he kisses her.

We walk into the house. I wrinkle my nose at the stale attic smell. There's a hint of something else, too, like furniture polish. Nana is in a recliner, and she claps her hands together when she sees us.

"Look at these babies!" she says, slowly getting up. She's wearing a sweatshirt with a kitten on the front—she and Mom have the same taste in clothes. Mom, Shelby, and I are kissed once again. Nana's cheek feels soft and saggy and a little cold next to mine.

"We brought you guys a little something," Mom says, handing Nana a red and green gift bag. It's a framed photograph of Shelby and me standing in front of the mantle at home in our Easter dresses. Nana sits it on the coffee table. The entire house is filled with pictures of me and Shelby and our cousins—too many pictures, really. Their frames look dusty in the light streaming through the curtains.

"They're growing so fast," Nana says. She leans toward me. "I bet this one has a boyfriend already."

I frown. Mom elbows me.

"I don't have a boyfriend!" Shelby says. "Look!" She holds up her Barbie head for Nana to inspect.

"That sure is pretty," Nana says. "Where's the rest of her?"

Shelby squishes her face up, confused.

Pop waddles over and takes out his wallet. "Let me give these girls a little Christmas money," he says. I know he's going to give us five dollars each, like he does every year. I thank him, and I really *am* thankful—cash is invaluable right now. Shelby immediately gives her money to Mom, unsure of what she should do with it.

We stand around for a moment. Mom and Pop discuss the nice weather, then Mom and Nana discuss Dad, which makes me want to put my hands over my ears and scream *la la la* like Shelby does when she's in the middle of a tantrum. Mom tells Nana that Shelby and I spent the weekend with Dad.

"Poor babies," Nana says. She clicks her tongue, then shakes her head at us. "Their world has been turned upside down." It makes me feel pathetic and sad, and for a moment I imagine Shelby and I dressed in rags, wandering the streets of Phoenix and stumbling up to Nana and begging her for a coin.

Mom's face gets a little red, and she changes the subject. "I was hoping you could show Dani your canning room. She's really into prepping these days."

I feel my eyes go wide. I'd been to Nana and Pop's house at least once every year, but I'd rarely journeyed past the living room and bathroom.

"Is that so?" Nana says. Her eyebrows are high on her forehead, near her puffy gray bangs, so she seems surprised, too. "Well, let's take a peek. It's nothing special, but I've been canning a long time."

We follow Nana and Pop to a small room with a washer and dryer in one corner and rows of wooden shelves mounted to the wall of the other. This room smells different than the rest of the house—like fabric softener and something else, something crisp and natural, similar to the way the dusty ground smells after a rain shower. When I walk fully into the room and get a good look at everything, I gasp. I can't help it.

I'd researched canning when I first stumbled upon Professor Prepared. It was the best way to store food, but with a limited amount of time and parents that seemed less than supportive, I had to settle for canned food from the grocery store. But I knew the basics: You needed clean Mason jars. You needed lids with two parts. And you preferably needed a garden. I knew Nana gardened, but I never expected *this*.

The shelves hold rows and rows of glass jars, and they seem to be sorted by color, like a vertical rainbow. There are labels plastered to the front of each one, and Nana's wobbly handwriting identifies the contents: *tomatoes, greens, cucumbers.* It looks like a photo that might appear on Professor Prepared's website. There's a little bit of sunlight coming through a small window, and it shines on the jars, making them glow. They look almost like treasure, and in a way, they are. Nana and Pop surely have enough food to last them months—maybe even a year.

"Been canning since I was a girl," Nana says, waving her wrinkled hands toward the shelves. "Never know what's in the food we eat nowadays, so it's good to be prepared."

My stomach feels warm—not the angry sort of warm I felt at Dad's yesterday, but a happy, understood kind of warm. Maybe I'm not so abnormal. Maybe I'm just like Nana. *Kindred spirits* as Ms. Paige would say.

"All kinds of pesticides in our food now," Pop says, tapping his walking stick against the floor.

"*Pest-in-sides?*" Shelby parrots, testing the word out.

"What's got you so interested in canning?" Nana asks. "Most kids your age like going through the drive thru."

Mom answers before I can, placing a hand on my shoulder. "She's going through a bit of a phase, we think. She's obsessed with Y2K. It's all she talks about."

The warm feeling in my stomach disappears, and I scowl up at Mom.

"Oh, that stuff about the computers?" Pop asks.

I suddenly feel tired, so I just nod, not bothering to explain that it's much bigger than that.

Nana draws closer to me. She rubs her chin, and her gaze drifts toward the ceiling, as though she's remembering something. "You know, when I was in school, only a little bit older than you, we had something similar. Everyone was afraid of nuclear weapons in those days. The teachers insisted we needed to be prepared."

Pop nods. He must be remembering the same thing.

"We had to watch this little video," Nana continues. "It was on a film reel. Cartoon of a turtle and monkey. *Duck and Cover* it was called. It told us to duck under our desks and cover our heads if they dropped the big one. It felt like we practiced every other week."

I smile. Of course, Nana's preparedness comes from world events. Just like mine.

"And do you know what I learned?" Nana asks. She bops Shelby on the nose.

"To be ready for anything?" I guess. After all, that's what I've learned by studying all the things that could go wrong—and probably will go wrong—on January 1st, 2000.

Nana laughs. "I learned that it was all a bunch of poppycock," she says. I feel my face fall. I even feel a little nauseous, like I just got off a ride at an amusement park. "Even if someone had dropped the big one, there was no way that hiding under a desk was going to save us. What a waste of time! And, you know, there'll always be something. War. Computers that stop working. Disease. You got to live your life without fear."

I swallow and nod my head, but that's not what I really want to do. I want to stomp my feet in Nana's canning room, shaking her precious organized jars. I want to scream at Mom that this isn't a phase. I want to tell Nana it isn't about being scared. It was never about being scared. It's about being prepared. It's about having a plan. It's about being *together.*

Instead, I take a deep breath and walk out of the canning room. I suppose I should be ashamed. This could be the last time I see my grandparents. But now that I've seen the canning room, I know they're more prepared than my family could ever be—regardless of whether or not Nana believes preparedness is poppycock.

The attic smell is back, filling my nostrils, and it makes me feel sick. "I'm ready to go home," I call over my shoulder to Mom.

Chapter Six

December 21st, 1999

10 Days Before

I've started growing a new crop on *Bounty Crescent*: brussel sprouts. They grow in pretty green clusters, and they sell for quite a bit when I take them into town. I'm gathering them in my pixelated basket when my computer dings. It's my instant messenger.

I put down my Game Grasp and head to my computer. There's a green blinking box telling me I have a message from Trinity. We've not spoken online since our project was complete. I groan, feeling heavier all of a sudden. My chair even rolls back a little.

Then I open the text box.

Trinity: Hey. You got a minute?

I'm tempted to just ignore the message, but curiosity wins out.

Dani: I guess.

There's some time before the next message comes through. I'm considering just logging out and shutting down my computer when she finally replies.

Trinity: I was wondering—do you have any extra Y2K supplies?

That's not what I expected. I squint at the screen as though I can see Trinity sitting at her own computer if I look hard enough. I'm sure she has a stupid pink bedroom with posters of boy bands and butterflies. I raise my hands to the keyboard.

Dani: Supplies???

Trinity: You know. Emergency food, maybe a big flashlight. A hazmat suit?

I feel my scowl twisting into a smile. Professor Prepared said this would happen, of course. He said that Y2K skeptics—like Trinity—would start to second guess themselves as the 31st drew near. They would start reaching out for help and acting apologetic.

Dani: I have everything I need for myself and my family. But if you go to Professor Prepared's website, you should be able to find the information you need. Good luck.

I want to exit out of instant messenger, and hear the satisfying door slam sound. But something is nagging me, and that something is guilt. It's a familiar sensation—I felt it minutes after stomping out of Nana and Pop's house yesterday.

Dani: If you don't have any luck, I might be able to spare a couple cans of food. That's it.

I imagine myself as one of the characters in *Bounty Crescent*, my basket full of cans, extending it to Trinity. Helping my townspeople. Being an important part of my community.

Trinity: Thank you so much!

I feel warm and happy for the space of one heartbeat before Trinity sends another message.

Trinity: Because I'm having a New Year's Eve party. It's Y2K themed, and I'll need some decorations. :)

I freeze, and my limbs feel like they're made of ice.

Trinity: Dad told me to make it really big since the whole thing is so ridiculous. We bought some caution tape. Dad is going to see about getting us a couple of gas masks from a guy he knows. Mom said we should call the snacks 'rations.' :D

I notice I'm pressing my hands into fists so tightly that my fingernails are making crescent moon-shaped marks on my palms. Why is it such a joke to Trinity? Why is it such a joke to *everyone?*

Trinity: I'd invite you, but I know you'll be super busy that night. Do you think maybe Riley would like to come?

I make a frustrated, gasping noise and close our chat window. Of course Riley would never come. Would he? And why do I care, anyway?

My mouse hovers over the button to shut down my computer, but I can't bring myself to do it. Instead, I go back to my instant messenger to see if he is online.

He is. I send a message.

Dani: Hi.

His response is so quick I jump a little. My desk chair rolls so far back that I have to scoot up to reach the keyboard again.

Riley: Hey! How are you?

Furious is the first word that comes to mind, but I don't want to explain it.

Dani: I'm good. How are you?

Another quick reply.

Riley: I'm good. It's kind of boring at home. I actually miss school. :)

I miss school, too, and in a weird way, I miss him. But I'm definitely not going to say that.

Dani: Doing anything fun for Christmas?

Riley: Not really. Usual family stuff. I've been reading, mostly. There's a new book out. It was supposed to be my Christmas present, but Mom gave it to me early.

I yawn. This is why I never talk to anyone. Carrying on conversations, online or in real life, is exhausting. But at least I'm less angry now.

Dani: That's nice. We're not really doing anything fun, either.

Riley: The book is pretty good, actually. The main character reminded me of someone, and then I realized it was you.

I feel myself blush.

Riley: She's like prepared for anything. And she knows a lot about zombies and survival. You should check it out.

I should thank him. I rack my brain trying to think of anyone who has taken my prepping seriously. My parents, the kids at school, Ms. Paige, Nana and Pop, Trinity—all of them have laughed at me or changed the subject or told me to knock it off. But not Riley.

Then I remember there are ten days standing between me and the end of the world. I have to worry about Mom, Dad, and Shelby. I have to worry about food and water and money and where we can go if things get bad in Phoenix. I don't have space in my brain to make Riley my friend and worry about him, too.

But when I think about never seeing Riley again, my stomach really hurts.

I log out of messenger and listen to the sound of the closing door. I shut down my computer, then head to my shelves. Examining each can of food, I check that the expiration date is far away, even though I know it is. Running my hands over the water jugs, I make sure there are no holes or dents in the plastic. I count and smooth out the money Dad and Pop gave me, then put it back neatly into the jar.

It's hard to do all of this with tears running down my cheeks.

Mom knocks a few hours later.

"What are you up to?" she asks. If she notices my red eyes or my blotchy cheeks, she doesn't say anything. She nudges the door wide open with her elbow.

"Nothing," I say, stepping away from my shelves.

Mom narrows her eyes at me. "Is there something you *should* be doing?"

I blink at her for a moment, confused, and then I remember. Mom was embarrassed after we abruptly left Nana and Pop's. "I know this has been a hard year, Dani," she said later, in the car, keeping one hand on the steering wheel and the other hand free to wag her finger at me. "But I didn't raise you—either one of you—to be rude. You don't even get to see your grandparents that often, and this is how you act?" She kept going on and on, and I was pretty annoyed, but also sort of comforted. She sounded like she used to, before the divorce.

"I'll call them when we get home and apologize," I'd said.

"Oh, you're going to do better than that," Mom said. "You're going to write a very long and detailed letter telling Nana and Pop how sorry you are. And, after Christmas, you're going to drop by their house and see if they need any chores done."

I quickly nodded in agreement, especially because I knew that, after Y2K, Mom wouldn't hold me to the whole chores thing. That doesn't give me an excuse for not working on the letter, though.

"I haven't started it," I say now. "But I will. I promise."

"Okay," Mom says. "I'm going to hold you to that." She shifts a little, and that's when I see she's holding something I instantly recognize: a blue and green glossy book. I groan.

"Come on," Mom says, walking fully into the room. She sits on my bed. "Just for a few minutes. Please?"

I slump, like my spine is made out of jelly. I know I'm being a pain, but Mom just smiles at me and pats the space on the bed next to her.

"I can do it from here," I say.

"Dani," Mom says. She raises her eyebrows.

All the sadness I felt earlier is gone. Now I'm just irritated. My face feels hot and itchy, and suddenly everything makes me mad—the weak smile on Mom's face, the fact that the corner of one of my drawings has come un-taped from the wall, the realization that the neck of my shirt feels too tight. I walk slowly over to the bed, like my ankles are shackled together.

The book Mom holds in her hands has a picture of a girl on the front. She's pretty, and she's dressed a little like Trinity with a bright pink t-shirt and clips in her hair. Her arms are crossed, and she's staring out a window with a sad expression on her face. The title above her head reads: *Talking to Your Preteen About Divorce: A Workbook for Families.* Mom insists we read a few pages together every Tuesday, and it's as miserable as going to the dentist.

Mom smells like cinnamon, and she has on a soft looking t-shirt, and suddenly I want to hug her. I want to snuggle in the crook of her arm, like I used to do when I was smaller, and have her gently rock me back and forth until my eyes get heavy. But I don't do any of that. I clasp my hands together instead. Mom opens to a page she's bookmarked and clears her throat. "Let's read the following scenario and brainstorm some solutions together," she says in the weird robotic voice she uses exclusively for reading out of this stupid workbook.

I look up at the ceiling and groan. Mom ignores me.

"Tamara's parents are divorced. Whenever Tamara's dad comes to pick her up, he fights with Tamara's mom. Sometimes they fight about money. Sometimes they fight about the custody schedule. Tamara feels very unloved. What should she do?" Mom heaves a deep breath, then looks at me.

I shrug, but I really want to knock the book out of Mom's hand, and watch it fall to the floor and shut so I don't have to hear about Tamara anymore. If I think really hard, I can still hear Mom and Dad's voices on the other side of the apartment door. I can still remember how I knew they were angry, even though I couldn't see their faces. I want to remind Mom that Tamara isn't real, and she doesn't matter. Nothing—even divorce—will matter in the days ahead.

"If I were Tamara, I would mind my own business," I say. "Are we done now?"

"Seriously, Dani," Mom says. She looks away from me and smooths her hand across the page. "What would you do?"

I decide to play along—anything to get Mom and this workbook out of my room. This is supposed to be my safe place, after all. "I would talk to both my parents and tell them how I feel," I mutter, mostly to my feet. That sounds like the kind of cheesy answer that would be in the workbook.

Mom smiles and nods. She turns the page. "Okay. I'm going to read a list of emotions. Let me know if you've felt any of them this past week. Do you understand?"

"Like, you want me to raise my hand or something?" I ask. Listening to her read is one thing. Actually having to move my body around and participate is another.

Mom shrugs. "If you want. But I think just a yes or no will do."

"Make it quick," I say. Mom raises an angry eyebrow at me, so I add, "Please."

Mom clears her throat again. "Happiness."

I think about the hearts that appeared over my cow's head in *Bounty Crescent*. "Sure," I say.

"Comfort," Mom says.

I think about how warm and soft my bed felt last night. "Yes," I say.

"Discomfort," Mom says.

Now I think about something weird. Last year, I read a book about the Salem Witch Trials. One of the sections described how the accusers would sometimes stack stones on the chest of the accused until he or she confessed to being a witch. I got sent to Ms. Paige for reading that book in class, even though I repeatedly told the teacher that it came from our school library.

And, at this moment, I feel like Mom is stacking stones on my chest. Accusing me of something, even though I don't know what it is. But I'm not going to confess.

"No," I say. "Not discomfort." It's a lie—I can still remember how quiet it became in Dad's apartment after Shelby got her wagon.

"Sadness?" Mom says. Out of the corner of my eye, I see her hand shake a little.

Another stone. I feel heavy, like pretty soon I'll sink into the mattress and through the floor and just keep going. "No," I say. "I'm fine." I try not to think of Riley's messages. I try not to imagine what will become of him and his family after January 1st.

"Anger," Mom says. She isn't looking at the book anymore. She's looking at me.

I think about Trinity's stupid party.

"No," I say, but I am flustered, and I feel like I can't get a full breath into my lungs. "I'm fine. Everything is fine. Can we stop this, please?" *There's no point in talking about this—everything will be completely different in eleven days*, I want to add. But I decide it will only make things worse, like it did with Dad. And Nana and Pop. And basically everyone else.

Mom shuts the notebook, and it makes a satisfying clapping noise. "I'm going to check on Shelby," she says. She doesn't sound angry, or happy. Just flat.

I nod, but I don't look at her. I look at my computer and watch the screensaver—black with zooming stars, like I'm flying through space—until I hear the door shut behind Mom. And then, I can finally breathe again.

Warm Holiday Wishes

By: Professor Prepared (professorprepared.com)

I know that we are coming upon a special time of year for many religions and cultures. Whether you celebrate Christmas, Chanukah, Kwanzaa, Winter Solstice, or if you're just looking forward to some well-deserved family time, I hope the coming days are restful and peaceful for you and yours.

Enjoy this time, preppers. Eat too much food. Hug your relatives a little too tightly. Spoil your children. Because the Y2K disaster looms on the horizon. Who knows what life will be like next winter—if we will have the time, resources, or mental capacity amid the chaos to stop and celebrate at all?

Now is not a time to be frightened, however. Now is a time to celebrate, secure in the knowledge that you are ready.

Stay safe, stay informed, and prepare for the worst. Good luck to you.

Still looking for that perfect gift? How about a gift card to the Professor Prepared Store?

Chapter Seven

December 24th, 1999

6 Days Before

Mom has gone overboard, as usual.

Christmas Eve dinner is always a big deal in our house but, this year, the food seems even more extravagant. Mom started cooking as soon as she woke up, and she only paused once when Shelby begged to use the potato masher. Even then, she hovered over her the entire time, never truly giving up control. For a moment, it was like the old Mom was back, and that was almost better than the promise of food. I'm not a natural in the kitchen like Mom, but I did ask if she needed my help. She waved me away, saying she was nearly done. And once everything is finished, there is a big ham, a basketful of crescent rolls, side dishes of mashed potatoes and green beans, and a full gravy boat. There is a chocolate cake for dessert, and Mom has decorated it with fondant holly leaves and berries.

The food looks amazing, but it doesn't make me forget that Dad isn't here. Tomorrow is Saturday, a day we're supposed to spend at Dad's apartment when he isn't busy working, but we're skipping this week because of Christmas. And, after last weekend, I'm sort of relieved. Every time I look at the *Bounty Crescent* poster he gave me—taped to the wall near my supply shelves—I feel angry all over again.

Shelby is centimeters away from sticking her finger into the cake's chocolate icing when Mom notices and gently smacks it away.

"Nope," she says. "You girls put on your nice clothes first, then we'll take pictures, then we'll eat."

Shelby and I groan simultaneously, but we're both pretty hungry, so we head to our bedrooms to change. I'm tempted to put on jeans and my least wrinkly button down, but I decide to wear something Mom would like for once. I go through my closet, finally settling on a black velvet dress with white tights and black shoes with buckles. The tights are itchy and the dress feels too heavy and hot to wear anywhere but indoors, but I'll suffer for a few hours. This is most likely my last Christmas Eve dinner. It's this thought that has me heading over to my vanity mirror—I'll probably never have another opportunity to use it, like Mom mentioned. I actually find a brush and use it on my hair, even find a white headband to complete the look.

Mom and Shelby are waiting for me in the living room. Shelby is wearing some frilly pink dress, and Mom is clipping a huge bow in her hair. She's also wearing sparkly gold Mary Janes, and she keeps clicking her heels together like Dorothy in *The Wizard of Oz*. Mom is wearing a red blazer and a gold hummingbird pin. She grins at me over one of her shoulder pads, and I can tell she's both surprised and happy. In my mind, I'm patting myself on the back.

"You look great, Dani," she says. I feel like I look silly, but Mom's compliment makes me feel sort of proud. Maybe that vanity mirror came in handy after all.

Shelby and I automatically head to the mantle to pose for our photo. Dad always said it was the place in the house with the best lighting, so that's where Mom photographed everything—Christmas Eve pictures, first day of school pictures, Easter pictures. But Mom shakes her head. "Let's try something different this year," she says, grabbing her bulky digital camera from the closet.

She ushers us outside. The winters in Phoenix aren't bad, not like the unbearable summers. Adults in Arizona like to say, *"If you can't handle our summers, you don't deserve our winters,"* and it's actually true—I've never had to worry about falling on ice or having the pipes in my house freeze like Professor Prepared sometimes describes on his website. But the sun is blinding year round, and I imme-diately shield my eyes when I step out the front door. Mom poses us next to the big cactus near our driveway. Shelby and I must look like a squinty mess, because she tells us to keep our eyes closed until she's ready to take the photo. I nod and do as she says, trying not to think about how we'll be meeting here beside this very cactus in six days to decide our next move.

"Put your arms around each other," Mom says behind the camera. "Okay, open your eyes and say cheese!"

Shelby stands on her tiptoes and stretches the word out, her tiny arms hugging me around the middle. The camera flashes.

"Don't you girls look pretty," someone says. It's our neighbor, Rich, who is tinkering with his old car over in his yard. He's usually out there every day—sometimes, I can even hear the metal clink of his tools at night through my bedroom window. "You want me to take one of all three of you?"

Mom looks a little embarrassed, but she nods. "Sure," she says. "That would be nice." Rich wipes his hands on his t-shirt and Mom hands him the camera carefully, as though it's made out of butterfly wings. Then she joins us, wrapping her arms around us both.

Afterward, we head back inside. Shelby goes straight for the chocolate cake, and Mom smacks her hands away again. "Real food first, then cake," she demands.

We sit at the table and pass the platters and dishes around until we all three have a little bit of everything. We'll have leftovers for days—which is unfortunate, as none of it will store well.

For a while, we just eat quietly. I can actually hear Shelby grunting as she chews. There's the shrill squeak of Mom's knife and fork on her ceramic plate. But I know the quiet won't last long. Soon Mom will ask her favorite question—the one she asks every Christmas Eve.

"So, let's talk about the best parts of this year," she says, like she just thought of it.

Shelby doesn't hesitate. "The cake!" she says, throwing her hands into the air.

"You haven't even had the cake yet," I say. I can't help it—my voice sounds frustrated. I know she's a kid, but sometimes Shelby makes absolutely no sense.

"So? I don't care," Shelby says, craning her neck to get a better view of the cake.

Mom chuckles. Then she puts down her fork, which is a relief because the squeaking was starting to give me a headache. I notice she touches the place on her finger where her wedding band used to be. I can remember the way it felt whenever I held Mom's hand, even though the last time that happened I was probably around Shelby's age. I can still feel the smooth gold band, the shiny stone that glinted when she moved and spoke and cooked.

"My favorite part of this year was all the time we spent together, of course," she says. "But I also landscaped the backyard all by myself. And I think it looks great. So, I'm really proud of that." She smiles at me, and it feels like hug, something just between the two of us. It is so easy to smile back. "Your turn, Dani," she adds.

I know I've had good moments this year, but for some reason, all I can think about are the ones that make my stomach give a familiar twist: the announcement after the Fourth of July fireworks, the photo of the Y2K bug in Dad's magazine, Trinity kicking her feet up on the news desk as though she were queen of the entire school, Nana calling my phase "poppycock."

Finally, I think of a positive one, so that's the one I decide to share. Last school year, in February, we had Career Day. There was a veterinarian, a dentist, a hairdresser, and a mechanic. And there was Dad, who actually took time off from work and brought a computer motherboard to show the class. Everyone was interested, and he wasn't as embarrassing as I had thought he would be. I actually felt sort of proud and accepted for once as my classmates passed around the motherboard and asked him questions.

Career Day was over by lunch, but Dad decided to sign me out. He called Mom, and she and Shelby met us at the Palm Mall. We had ice cream, and then we walked past the stores, talking and laughing and enjoying how empty it was during the day. Mom and Dad bought Shelby a glittery unicorn slap bracelet and me a scary book about a ventriloquist dummy that came to life. There were no arguments. There was no impending doom. There was just us, and I felt happy and light enough to fly.

I don't even get to finish telling Mom all of this before she begins to cry. Tears ruin her eye makeup, and I notice a smudge somehow lands on her nice red blazer. She reaches over and grabs my hand, squeezing my fingers together.

"That was one of my favorite days, too," she says. Her voice is hoarse and small.

And then we notice Shelby isn't in her seat any longer. We turn to find her standing next to the cake, her hands and chin covered in blobs of chocolate icing.

Chapter Eight

December 25th, 1999

5 Days Before

I'm surprised when Mom, not Shelby, wakes me up the next morning.

"Time to see what Santa brought," Mom whispers, sweeping a piece of hair away from my face. We both know I don't believe in Santa. I stopped when I was younger than Shelby, even. I don't remember it happening but, to hear Mom tell it, one Christmas I noticed that she and Santa used the same wrapping paper. After that, I couldn't be convinced. Still, I always put on a good show for my sister's sake. "You girls really slept in this year. I think Shelby might have crashed after all that sugar."

We laugh, and Mom pats my arm. It feels so nice and normal that I want to beg her to stay here with me and let Shelby sleep a little bit longer. She squeezes my shoulder, though, and heads to Shelby's room.

In the living room, the presents are perfectly stacked around the tree. The cookies Shelby left for Santa have disappeared except for one, which has a Mom-sized bite on the corner. Mom, once again, says we have to eat before we do anything else—scrambled eggs and toast for Shelby, Lucky Spangles for me.

"Is it time for presents now?" Shelby asks after nearly inhaling her breakfast. There's a smear of jam on her cheek, and her hair is wild and sticking up in many directions around her face.

Mom nods, and Shelby races out of the kitchen to the Christmas tree. Mom barely has enough time to get her camera out before Shelby claws into her first present—a pair of light-up sneakers. I think about how difficult it will be to travel in secret if Shelby wears those. Maybe I could camouflage them with some mud.

"Go on, Dani," Mom says, nudging me toward my own present pile. "Don't let Shelby have all the fun."

Half an hour later, Shelby and I are sitting in heaps of discarded wrapping paper, and all I can think about is Dad. That was typically his job—he'd sweep in with a trash bag, and we'd toss wads of paper in his direction like basketballs. Shelby has unwrapped so many toys I've lost count—Barbies and board games and glossy picture books. I've done pretty well myself—another small stack of cash, a pair of hiking boots that will certainly come in handy, a fruity smelling makeup palette that I'll likely never open. We're down to one present each, and Mom insisted we save this gift for last.

She has her camera pointed at us, the lens making her face look like she has one giant fish eye. "All right," she says. "Go ahead and open."

I can hear the noise of Shelby ripping into her present, but I take my time with mine. It's an odd shape, and I tear the tape from the edges first. When the wrapping paper falls to the floor, I realize I'm holding a pair of black and red mouse ears. I glance beside me, at Shelby, who is hugging her unwrapped gift—a large Minnie Mouse.

The camera flashes, momentarily blinding me. "Guess where we're going this summer?" Mom asks. For a moment, my head swims—from the camera flash and from confusion. But Shelby catches on before I do. She stands up, screams, and drops the Minnie Mouse on the floor.

"Disney World?" she asks, breathless. Mom nods, and I can only watch as Shelby's bare feet bounce around on the carpet. "Disney World!" she exclaims, her face pointed up at the ceiling. She runs to Mom, who sweeps her up in a hug.

But I can't move. I'm frozen on the floor, holding the mouse ears. My hands are starting to feel sweaty. I imagine them drenching the mouse ears and dripping onto the floor.

"We're going to see Cinderella," Shelby says into Mom's neck. "And Snow White. And Daisy. And Peter Pan!"

Mom nods at each name Shelby says, but her eyes are on me. She's smiling, but it's a wobbly smile, the one she uses when she's nervous but trying to pretend she's not. On the Fourth of July, when she turned around and gazed at Shelby and me from the passenger seat and asked if we had any questions, she was wearing the same exact smile. "Are you excited, Dani?" she asks.

I don't feel frozen anymore; I feel angry. My stomach feels hollow and hot. I can remember Mom brushing off the Y2K article in Dad's computer magazine. I can remember how exasperated she looked the last time she caught me looking over my supplies. I can remember her words from a few days ago, standing at the stove with Shelby. *Can you knock it off with that doomsday talk for one night?*

She didn't want to plan for Y2K, but she planned for this. How can she promise something that likely won't happen? How can she get Shelby so excited for Disney World when, in a few months' time, Disney World might not even exist?

I remember how tense the situation became at Dad's, so I force myself to swallow the lump in my throat. "Sounds great," I say instead, sitting the mouse ears on top of the makeup. Might as well stack the useless things together. "I'm going to get a trash bag for the wrapping paper."

That evening, I'm reading over Professor Prepared's blog post on water purification. I feel slightly panicked, as we don't have any of the supplies he's described. On our last trip to the grocery store, Mom told me that unscented bleach didn't exist, but I think she was lying. Yet another reason to be angry with her.

There's a soft rap at the door and, almost on cue, Mom sticks her head in.

"What are you up to?" she asks.

"Nothing," I say, but she knows what I'm looking at. She's seen the website many times. I hear her huff out a sigh, but she doesn't mention it.

"Shelby and I are watching *It's a Wonderful Life*," Mom says instead. "Why don't you come and sit with us?"

"That movie is boring," I say, scrolling down the webpage.

"Dani," Mom says. "Please?"

I sigh, and shut down my computer. The lights are off in the living room. There is only the glow of the black-and-white movie on the television screen and the red and green of the lights on the Christmas tree, which now looks kind of sad without any presents. Shelby is balled up on one side of the sofa, chewing her thumb. She's clutching her Minnie Mouse in one arm and her eyes look heavy. Mom snuggles next to her, in the middle, pulling a throw blanket with reindeer on it across her lap. I sink into the far side of the sofa. Onscreen, George Bailey is standing on a bridge, pleading for his life back.

In a few minutes, I hear Shelby's honking snore. So does Mom, because she turns to me.

"I know you're not happy about the Disney World trip," Mom says. "But, believe me, nothing is going to happen. And even if something did happen, you know I would take care of you girls. Right?"

I want to laugh. How can Mom take care of us? Mom, who has never read Professor Prepared's website. Mom, who thinks Y2K is a "phase." Mom, who bakes cakes and cries when she's happy and thinks about things like Disney World. Mom, who hasn't been her old self in months.

"When it happens, we'll be ready," I say. "But it's because of how prepared *I* am."

Even in the dark, I can see Mom looks hurt. But she doesn't say anything. She just reaches over and intertwines her fingers with mine. I grip her bare ring finger, but if she notices, she doesn't mention it. She just holds my hand until the credits roll.

Some Final Advice and a Farewell

By: Professor Prepared (professorprepared.com)

Readers, by this time tomorrow, we will surely live in a new world.

Our lives will immediately divide into two distinct phases—life before December 31st, 1999, and life after December 31st, 1999. It is frightening to be on the precipice of so much change. But if you're a faithful reader of this website, your knowledge and preparation will probably save your life and the lives of your loved ones. Stay vigilant, but give yourself a pat on the back.

I have wracked my brain trying to come up with something profound to share with all of you as this will likely be my last post to this website. The internet, of course, will be one of the first conveniences to disappear in the wake of the Y2K disaster. I suppose a long, tearful goodbye post would be fitting; however, I decided to stick to what I do best—dispensing advice.

By now you know about bugging out, canning and storing food, water storage and purification, and many other catastrophe-related topics. But there is perhaps no information more important than this: Have a Plan B. And C. And D. And E. An event like Y2K has a multitude of possibilities. Plan for everything. And then, when you feel like you've planned for everything, plan some more. You will certainly regret planning too little, but I know of no one who regrets planning too much.

I will spend today practicing a final round of drills with my family, ensuring all our food and water is stored correctly, and keeping up with news around the world. I'll remain skeptical of what I see and hear. I urge you to do the same.

In closing, expect for everything to change. Except for the Postal Service. I do believe they'll continue to get to us, despite "snow or heat or gloom of night," as the creed says. So, if you'd like to send a donation, my P.O. box will remain open.

One last time: stay safe, stay informed, and prepare for the worst. Good luck to you.

Chapter Nine

December 30th, 1999

1 Day Before

Mom, Shelby, and I are gathered around the kitchen table. I've repurposed my sketchbook into a checklist, and as I read each item, I glance up at Mom. She's slumped forward, her chin resting on her hand.

"And if we shelter in place, we'll have to make sure we have good lighting at the front of the house. You know, if the electricity stays on," I say.

"We're good there," Mom says.

"How do you know?" I ask.

Shelby holds up her hands. She's stuck Barbie high heels on two of her fingers, and she walks them across the table and hums under her breath.

Mom blinks and her neck looks flushed and red, like it does before she gets angry with me. But she doesn't yell. She takes a deep breath instead, then says, "I changed the bulb on the front porch earlier this month, when we were putting up Christmas lights."

I nod, and make a heavy, dark check in my sketchbook. "Okay, good. What about the smoke detectors? They're charged, right? They've been working correctly?"

Shelby clicks her tongue in time with the high heels. Even over the noise, I can hear Mom sigh again.

"Yes," she says. "Of course I make sure the smoke detectors are working, Dani."

"Just going through the checklist," I say.

Shelby starts singing some made-up song under her breath, something about legs going to the mall.

"Do we have locks on the windows?"

"Going to the mall in my high heels…"

"Yes," Mom says. "And the front door. And the patio door."

"One thing at a time," I say.

"Going to see my boyfriend at the ma-aaallll…" Shelby holds out the final note, clomping the shoes against the table in a grand finale.

"Knock it off," I tell her. The space between my eyes is starting to ache. Mom looks as though she's got a headache, too, because she's rubbing her temples.

"Do we really need to do this right now?" Mom asks.

I want to remind her that New Year's Eve is tomorrow. That there is no better time. But I close the cover of my notebook and decide to complete the checklist on my own.

"Let's do something else," I say. "Let's practice meeting up."

"Is that really something we need to practice?" Mom asks. She isn't looking at me—she's trying to get something off of Shelby's face with her thumb. Shelby is frowning and pushing her away and making an unhappy grunting noise. "We've practiced meeting up a few times now."

"Yes," I say. "Professor Prepared says—"

Mom gives her loudest sigh yet and stands up. She reaches for Shelby's hand.

"What are we doing?" Shelby asks.

The red on Mom's neck has spread to her chin and disappears down the front of her cheetah sweatshirt, but her voice is calm when she speaks. "We're going to practice Dani's drill. You know, like the fire drills you have at school?"

Shelby gasps. "The fire truck is coming?"

I shake my head, and Shelby's shoulders slump. I lead the way through the front door and stand by the saguaro cactus beside our driveway. Dad once estimated it was around fifteen feet tall, and it has two spindly arms that reach toward the sky. It's the perfect landmark. Mom and Shelby seem to be dragging their feet, but they eventually join me.

"So, this is where we will head at midnight so that we're all together," I say. "Dad too."

Mom clears her throat, then begins to say something. But Shelby interrupts.

"I want to meet next to the pig!" Shelby says, her voice transforming to a whine. She points to one of Mom's lawn statues—a copper javelina. It's ridiculous, because we once saw a *real* javelina eating out of our trash, and Shelby cried for days because she was terrified it was going to come back.

"No," I say. "This is where we are planning on meeting. It's too late to change it now."

Shelby's bottom lip trembles. "The pig!" she shouts. She crosses her arms and makes the grunting sound from earlier.

"Does it really matter, Dani?" Mom asks. She tilts her head one way, then another, like she's trying to pop her neck. "Can't we just meet next to the javelina?"

I want to throw a tantrum like Shelby. I want to chuck my sketchbook into the street. I want to scream and stomp my feet and hold my breath until I can't hold it anymore. But then I notice our neighbor, Rich, in his front yard. He waves at us, his eyebrows raised like he's confused by our impromptu family gathering. The hood of his dumb old car is open, and it's making a grumbly noise which reminds me of Pop clearing his throat.

I can tell Mom is embarrassed because she ducks her head a little. "Let's wrap this up," she says. "Shelby obviously needs a nap."

"The cactus is our meeting place," I say. "End of discussion."

Mom puts Shelby down for a nap, then meets me in the garage. I stand next to the car with a stopwatch while she loads duffel bags full of clothes and canned goods into the trunk.

"You have to do it faster than that," I say. "What if this was an emergency?"

Mom stops loading and glares at me. "A little help would be nice," she says.

"I'm timing," I say, waving the stopwatch to remind her. "We should probably let Dad do this part if it comes down to it. He's got longer arms, so maybe he'll be faster."

Mom slams the trunk closed. "Speaking of your dad, have you talked to him?"

I shake my head. Mom makes a quiet noise, something between a groan and a laugh.

"Do you even know if he's going to be here tomorrow?"

"He said he would try," I say. Something about Mom's question makes me feel light headed.

Mom reaches for me and picks a piece of lint off my shirt. "I would maybe remind him of that obligation," she says. "And why don't you do something fun for a few minutes? Maybe play *Bounty Crescent*. Take a nap like Shelby. I'll look over that checklist, if you want."

I hug the sketchbook to my chest. "No, I've got it," I say. But my head still feels swimmy, and lying down suddenly sounds like a good idea. "I might take a nap, though. It never hurts to be well rested."

Mom smiles at me, but her eyes look sort of sad.

I sleep too long and have strange dreams of the Y2K bug smiling down at me from my bedroom ceiling, its eyes glowing with neon ones and zeroes. When I gasp myself awake, I see the purplish orange of evening outside my window. I'm trying to shake away the image of the bug, rubbing my eyes with my fists, then I remember—I need to talk to Dad.

He had to work today—last minute Y2K preparation, like it will do any good—but he should be home
by now. Things are still weird between us, though, so I
decide not to call him. I switch on my computer and pull
up my instant messenger.

"Hey," I type to his avatar—the generic, blank outline
of a head and shoulders. A text box near the top of the
screen reminds me he is offline and might not get the
message. I keep typing anyway. *"Just reminding you that
tomorrow is New Year's Eve. You said you'd try to be here with us.
We're meeting by the big cactus."*

I close the chat window and look at my other con-
tacts. Trinity's away message reads: *Getting ready to party
like it's 1999!* Natalie has a new away message, too. I
narrow my eyes and read it: *Your BFF Lauren wuz here!
Luv ya! :)*

Lauren?

And then I notice Natalie's avatar has changed. It
used to be a snapshot from our fifth-grade field trip to
the Heard Museum. Mom was one of the chaperones, so
she took the picture. We were standing together near the
museum's entrance, our heads tilted toward each other.
I was holding up my fingers, creating bunny ears behind
Natalie's baseball cap.

Now it's a photo of Natalie and a different girl. They
both look like they're wearing eyeliner. Their heads are
angled different ways, but they're both looking into the
camera. Their lips are puckered, like they're about to
kiss someone.

I take a deep breath and try not to let it hurt. *It doesn't
matter*, I tell myself. *Everything is changing tomorrow.* But my

stomach feels like it is turning summersaults, and my vision blurs with tears. I rub my eyes with my fists and square my shoulders. *It doesn't matter*, I tell myself again. I swallow the tickling sensation in my throat and keep breathing deeply until my tears are gone.

I notice Riley is online. I click on his name.

I've typed "hi" and my finger is hovering over the *send* button, then my eyes drift to the date and time at the bottom left of the screen. 7:24 PM on December 30th, 1999.

It's too late for that, I decide. It's too late to check on Riley. It's too late to be angry at Natalie, or to wish she never moved away, or try to make her *my* best friend again. It's too late to convince Trinity that the theme for her party is stupid. It's too late for everything. I shut down my computer.

Chapter Ten

December 31st, 1999

The Day

I have one remaining bowl of Lucky Spangles, which is pretty convenient.

The last bit of cereal is always the best, because the marshmallow bits have turned to dust. They cling to the boring wheat pieces and turn the milk all sorts of interesting colors. I take my time pouring in the cereal, finding all the different shapes—green balloons, pink stars, dusty halves of rainbows. I take my bowl to the kitchen table, ready to enjoy one last normal morning.

And then the oven gives a shrill beep, and I jump.

Mom strolls into the kitchen. She opens the oven door, maneuvers a toothpick into whatever is inside, then shakes her head. She closes the oven door again.

"What're you making?" I ask around my Lucky Spangles.

"A cake," Mom says. "For tonight."

"Seriously?" I ask before I can stop myself. We need unscented bleach and N95 masks and rubber gloves and more canned food. We definitely do not need cake.

Mom holds up a finger. "And I got these," she says, retrieving a plastic grocery bag from the top of the refrigerator. I watch, hoping that she'll pull out something useful. She dumps three pairs of what appear to be plastic sunglasses on the table in front of me.

I shrug. "Glasses? I mean, they might come in handy if—"

"Not just any glasses," Mom says. She slips a pair onto her face, and I discover they're purely decorative. The glasses are in the shape of the number 2000, and the middle zeroes serve as the eye holes. "Fun, huh?"

"Mom," I groan.

Mom grabs another pair of the glasses and tosses them my way. I catch them before they fall into my cereal. "Don't look at me like that," she says. "I've let you make a plan for if things go wrong, so this is my plan for if things go *right*. We'll eat cake and wear funny glasses and watch the ball drop. If Shelby can stay up that long."

I don't want to spend my last normal morning arguing with my mom, so I just nod.

"And if the news is any indication, everything is going right," Mom adds. "It's already the year 2000 in Australia and Japan. The reporter said everything went perfectly, no glitches, no hiccups. Their computers turned right over just like they were supposed to."

"Professor Prepared says to stay skeptical," I say.

"Of course he does," Mom says. "Make sure you rinse out your bowl before you put it in the sink."

When I return to my bedroom, my instant messenger is flashing.

Suddenly, I remember Trinity's Y2K party, and I feel my cheeks warm. She's probably telling me about her tacky decorations or her stupid gas masks. I don't have time for her, not today of all days. I march over to my computer, prepared to log out of everything and shut it off for the day—shut it off for good—when I see the message isn't from Trinity.

It's from Dad.

Dad: Dani, you there?

I sink into my desk chair, typing frantically, afraid he'll disappear before I can respond.

Dani: Yeah, I'm here. Did you get my message?

There's a pause, and for a moment I'm afraid he's logged off. The icon next to his avatar still says he's online, so I wait.

Dad: I'm sorry, kiddo. My supervisor wants me to stay here tonight to make sure all the computers roll over correctly. I don't have any choice.

When Mom and Dad told us their news on the Fourth of July, I was too surprised and then too angry to cry. I instead felt like I was frozen and the world was moving around me, but I wasn't a part of it. Mom and Dad were talking at us, and Shelby was wiggling in her booster seat, but I was stuck. Still there, still existing. Just stuck.

That's how I feel when I read and reread Dad's words.

Dad: I wouldn't stay if I wasn't positive that everything was going to be one hundred percent okay. And it will be. Nothing bad will happen tonight, Dani. Okay?

Out of the corner of my eye, I can see Mom stick her head into my bedroom. "And China is officially in the new millennium," she says. "No problems there, either."

"Dad's not coming," I say. I try to turn my head toward her, but I can't pull my eyes away from the screen.

I hear Mom come into the room, feel her standing next to me. She looks at the computer screen, too.

"Oh, Dani," she says.

I blink, hard, and am finally able to look away from the monitor and toward her. "Maybe we can meet him at the office," I say. I remember Professor Prepared's words—always have a Plan B. "We would have to pack all the supplies. And we'd have to make sure Shelby is somewhat awake. Maybe I can ask Dad to make sure her wagon is there. He'd probably have to go home and get it, though. But do you think we could shelter in place at his office? It's probably not a secure building, is it?" I'm trying to remember the way Dad's office looked on the few times we visited him at work. I can remember a water cooler and a loud copy machine and an elevator that said "going up" when you pressed a button. I'm suddenly angry with myself for not remembering more, for not planning for this scenario.

As I'm speaking, Mom's face is getting sadder and sadder. She leans forward, and I feel her kiss the top of my head. "I don't think going to Dad will be possible, sweetheart," she says. "I'm sorry."

I nod, and then, before I can change my mind, I log out of my instant messenger. Dad won't be part of my plans tonight. Saying that, even in my own head, makes my hands feel sweaty. But I still have Mom and Shelby.

I'm still prepared to keep them safe. And if I can keep them safe, then maybe we can reunite with Dad and be safe together.

"Change of plans," Mom says, squeezing my shoulder. "We do whatever you want. If you want to meet outside by the big cactus at midnight, that's what we'll do. The ball drop is boring anyway. All those crowds and anchors talking—and all that *kissing*." She makes a gagging noise, but I remember how she used to give all three of us— me, Shelby, and Dad—a peck on the cheek after the ball dropped.

"Okay," I say. I still feel frozen. My movements feel stiff and slow, as if I'm on the moon.

Mom gives me one last squeeze. "It would be a shame to throw out the cake, though," she says.

Thirty minutes to midnight. I've counted and reorganized the supplies on my shelves. I've gone back over the checklist. I've tested the lights in every room of the house, turned the flashlights on and off. I've checked the dial tone on the phones, noted that the closest one to me is in a nook just outside my bedroom. I've reviewed the procedures with Mom and then with Shelby, who buried her face in the sofa and said she didn't want to talk anymore. Now there's nothing to do but wait.

So, I'm in my bedroom with my Game Grasp and a piece of cake. Mom has even let me have the fondant Baby New Year she made for the topper. He has a monocle and a top hat and a moustache that looks suspiciously like the one on Professor Prepared's avatar.

The numbness from Dad's message has faded a little, but my body still feels heavy, like I spent the day before running uphill or trying to walk fast on sand. I don't feel nervous or scared, though. I feel clear-headed, like I've crammed for a test that I know I'm going to ace. But I feel sad at this moment, too, because the time has come to say goodbye to my *Bounty Crescent* farm.

I give my cow a quick milking. I brush her spotted coat, make sure her stall is stuffed with hay. By tapping the buttons on my Game Grasp several times in a row, I throw feed to my chickens. I pull the watering can from my inventory and make sure my tulips are watered. I dig up a pesky thatch of weeds that has grown near my pear tree. For the final time, I collect a harvest from my garden: tomatoes, then some peas and a few stalks of corn. I take my bounty into town and hand it to the owner of the general store.

"Thank you," says the speech bubble above the owner's head. "The townspeople will appreciate such hearty crops." He even winks and tips his straw hat to show his appreciation.

And even though I know it's silly, even though I know they are not real, I hope they'll be okay. My animals. My flowers. The townspeople. I switch off my Game Grasp.

I'm polishing off my cake when Mom comes into my room. She's carrying Shelby on her hip, even though we've told her many times that she's too big to pack around. Shelby's head is flopped on Mom's shoulder, and her eyes are droopy.

"Two minutes to go," Mom says. "Want to head outside?"

"We're going outside?" Shelby asks groggily.

"We're meeting at the cactus, remember?" Mom says.

"No, I want to meet at the pig," Shelby says, but she starts to snore before we've even left my bedroom.

On our way out, we pass the television set. Onscreen, there's a big crowd in Time Square, hugging one another and brushing confetti from their hair. New York is hours ahead of Phoenix; it looks like nothing catastrophic happened when they rang in the New Year. But I've been reading Professor Prepared long enough to know that everything can be manipulated. I remain skeptical, just as he said.

The cactus's arms are still reaching upward, of course, but tonight, in the dark, it looks different. The cactus looks like it's celebrating. It looks like it's ready for anything, even our imminent doom. For a moment, I just stare at it and the stars overhead. Whatever happens next, wherever my family goes, I hope I'll still be able to see the sky, the stars. I hope the chaos of what's to come won't erase the beauty of this moment. Seeing Mom and Shelby next to me, knowing that they are here and safe and whole, creates a warm tingling in my chest. There's a twinge of panic, too, when I remember Dad isn't with us but is instead holed up in an office building with a layout I can't remember. *Will he be stuck when the elevators no longer work? How will he escape the looters and get back to us?* I take a deep breath and push those worries to the side—for now. I've got to stay calm and handle one thing at a time.

Mom looks at her watch, the face glowing neon green in the dark. "I think we can start counting down," she says, shifting Shelby a little on her hip. "Ten," she starts.

"Nine," I say.

"Eight," we say together.

As we continue, I strain my ears for any sign of distress—people screaming or the sizzle of failing electricity or the clink of machinery across the city grinding to a halt. Maybe, in the worst-case scenario, the noise of explosions and crashes. But there's nothing but the hoot of owls.

"Happy New Year," Mom whispers when there are no more numbers left.

Nothing. There's stars and owls and the cactus and quiet. Around us, the world is still.

Nothing. Nothing has happened. Nothing is happening.

I'm surprised when the tears come. I feel my face crumpling. A noise comes out of me—the kind of wailing I've only heard out of Shelby during her worst tantrums. My vision blurs, but I can still make out the outline of Mom. I see her reaching for me with her free arm. She's saying something, but my sobbing drowns it out.

Then, from somewhere behind me, there's a *bang* so startling and loud that it seems to echo inside my skull. Mom is squeezing my hand, *hard*. Shelby is suddenly awake and screaming. I'm leaping toward both of them and burying myself in Mom's chest and arms. I'm both terrified and a little excited and all I can think is *I knew it.*

I knew it.

504 Error Gateway Time-Out

professorprepared.com's server IP address could not be found. Please ensure you have entered the web address correctly or try again later.

Chapter Eleven

January 1st, 2000

"**I**'m sorry!"

The voice is coming from across the lawn: Rich. I turn, and even through my tears I can see that he is sprinting toward us, waving his hands in front of him.

"I am so, so sorry." He reaches forward, like he wants to touch my shoulder, but he must think better of it because he pulls his arm away and holds it down at his side. "I'm off work tomorrow, so I thought I would come out with my flashlight and work on the car a little bit." He gestures behind him, where I can see the silhouette of the rusty old car in the moonlight. A flashlight is sitting on the hood, shining toward the ground. "I didn't expect it to backfire. And I didn't know anyone was out here. Again, I am so sorry I scared you guys." My vision has finally cleared enough to really see a bit of his face in the darkness—his eyes are big and his hands are shaking. He is really sorry. I feel sorry for him. I feel sorry for both of us.

I try to say something, to let him know he is forgiven, but every time I open my mouth a strangled whine comes out. I'm so embarrassed. I can't remember the last time I actually cried in front of other people. And crying is such a waste of time—it does nothing, helps no one.

On Mom's hip, Shelby appears to be wide awake, the collar of Mom's shirt clutched in her tiny fist. Shelby looks between me and Rich, then points her finger at him. "Your car is mean!" she shouts.

Mom pushes Shelby's finger down. "It's all right, Rich. I think we're all just a little on edge tonight." She looks toward me but I still can't talk. I only nod, then wipe my running nose with the sleeve of my hoodie.

"I hope you girls will be okay," Rich says. "Happy New Year."

"Happy New Year," Mom says. "I think it's time for us to turn in."

Once we're back in the house, Mom takes Shelby to her bedroom. Through the wall, I can hear Shelby arguing that she's not tired and Mom reminding her that it is very, very late. I sink into the living room sofa and stare at the television. There's a red-headed comedian in Times Square with a microphone. She's telling her co-hosts that she's planning on starting the seafood diet in the new year.

"Seafood diet?" some man with a bad toupee asks.

"If I see food, I'm going to eat it!" she says, and her co-hosts laugh like it's the funniest joke they've ever heard. A sob bursts out of me, and I clap my hands over my mouth.

The scene on the television screen changes—this time to a singer in an expensive and impractical-looking fur coat. She's singing into a microphone—some song about partying all night. I'm not paying close attention to the lyrics. The camera pans out, showing an enormous crowd circling the singer's stage. Audience members clap and kiss and blow into horns. They wear shiny top hats and feather boas and even some of those stupid 2000 sunglasses that Mom brought home from the store.

The clock on the wall tells me it is 12:21. Twenty four hours ago, I believed that, at this time, my family would be huddling together deciding what to do next. Maybe we would put our supplies in the car and head out. Maybe we would barricade our doors and windows and huddle together inside. Maybe we would all gather around the clock radio in Mom and Dad's bedroom— or I guess just Mom's bedroom, now—and listen to an emergency broadcast. But nothing happened. That's good, isn't it?

So why can't I stop crying?

When I hear Mom shutting Shelby's bedroom door, I wipe the tears from my cheeks and try to breathe normally. She sits next to me on the sofa. "All it took was one reading of *Goodnight Moon* and she was out," Mom says. Then she reaches over and squeezes my knee. "You want to talk about it, Dani?" she asks.

I only shake my head, afraid that doing more than that will cause me to cry again.

On the TV screen, the hosts are telling the viewers goodnight atop the cheers and commotion of Times Square. Mom reaches for the remote on the coffee table and turns the television off. She doesn't ask any more questions, just lets it go, and I'm reminded, once again, of how different she is now. She pushes herself off the sofa. "We need to head to bed as well. Maybe tomorrow you'll feel a lot better."

I know what she says isn't true, but I head to my room anyway. I try not to look at the shelves full of cans and water jugs and neatly folded dollar bills as I get ready for bed.

When I wake up, it's the middle of the day. I can tell because the sun is shining too brightly through my window. It bounces off the aluminum cans on the shelves, creating a silver pattern that stretches around the room. I stare at it and think about all my hard work. All my planning. And for what? When I went to bed, my face felt puffy and full of pressure, like I could cry at any moment. Today, there's none of that. My stomach feels hot and twisty, and all I want to do is run over to the shelves and kick them, flinging all the stuff to the ground. Then I want to stomp on everything and scream and scream and scream.

But I don't do any of that. There's a strange, sour taste in my mouth, so I get out of bed and brush my teeth. Then I walk into the living room.

There's a kid's show on television—a bunch of people in tiger costumes jumping rope. Shelby is sitting cross-legged on the carpet, inches from the screen, her eyes wide as she takes it all in. Mom has told her countless times not to sit so close. "You're going to hurt your eyes!" she would say. She even threatened to put a baby gate around the television so Shelby wouldn't be able to go near it. I roll my eyes as I walk past Shelby and into the kitchen. Mom is sitting at the table leafing through the newspaper.

Mom looks up at me and smiles. "Good morning," she says, patting the empty chair next to her. "Or should I say good afternoon?"

I don't answer, but I do slide into the chair.

"I was just reading about a new restaurant opening downtown," Mom continues, jabbing her finger at the article in the paper. "You come in with a group and eat in total darkness. Can you believe that?"

I can tell she's trying to distract me, so I'm determined not to comment on her dumb article. "Shelby is sitting way too close to the TV," I say instead.

Mom waves her hand in the direction of the living room. "She'll be all right," she says. Then she nods toward the center of the table. "There's some banana bread there if you're hungry. Came out of the oven not that long ago. It might still be warm."

It hits me, then: this isn't right. We're supposed to all be together—Mom, Dad, Shelby and me. We're supposed to be thriving, doing so much better than anyone else because I had a plan. Instead, we're split apart. Dad is at his dingy apartment with his paper plates or maybe still in his stupid office—I'm not sure which, since he didn't even call and check in after New Year's. Shelby is in her own world in front of the television. Mom is ignoring it and making banana bread instead. This wasn't what was supposed to happen.

"I don't want your dumb banana bread," I say. I know I'm the one who said it, but my voice sounds unfamiliar—loud and mean. I don't talk to my Mom this way. I don't talk to anyone this way.

Mom gasps. "Danielle Collier—-"

"And I think you should say something to Shelby. In fact, I think you should go back to acting the way you did before the divorce. You know, like our mom." I'm yelling, and I don't yell often. I suddenly feel winded, like I'm in a swimming pool and I've just come up for air. I suck in a deep breath. "And I'm sorry I can't just eat cakes and pretend that everything is normal. I'm not normal. Just ask Dad. He made that clear the last time I was at his apartment."

My hand is clenched into a fist on the table. Mom tries to reach over and hold it, but I pull it away.

"I didn't expect this to happen," I say, and now I'm crying again. But I know these tears are different. These are angry tears. I feel like I could grab the banana bread from the center of the table and smash it to crumbs with my bare hands. I feel like I could run into my bedroom, grab all the cans from my shelves, and bust out every window in our house.

"You didn't expect what to happen?" Mom asks. Her voice is so quiet, almost a whisper.

"Everything was supposed to change," I say. "And we were supposed to go back to the way we were before."

When I look at Mom, her cheeks are wet and red. She reaches for me. "Come on," she says, standing. "I think you should go lie down."

I want to argue with her and smack her hands away and tell her I just woke up, but I suddenly feel exhausted, as if everything has been drained from me. I follow her on wobbly legs past Shelby who is still sitting too close to the TV and back into my bedroom. I lie down, and Mom leaves, but returns later with a damp, warm washcloth. She settles it over my eyes and the tops of my cheeks, and I feel an immediate relief.

"Take a minute," Mom says. I can't see her anymore, but I can feel her hovering over me. "Close your eyes and calm down. Okay?"

I nod, then I hear my bedroom door click shut.

The next thing I hear is the tapping of the telephone cord hitting the wall outside my room. I know Mom is standing just outside, in the nook, and she's on the phone. I hear snippets of conversation, and I immediately know who she is speaking with.

"I think you should make some time to come over tomorrow," Mom says. I can picture her with the receiver to her ear, pacing as far as the cord will allow. "She really needs you. She really needs both of us, I think."

I try to imagine Dad's reaction on the other end of the line, but I come up blank.

Chapter Twelve

January 2nd, 2000

2 Days After

Shelby has been pouting all morning. She keeps it up, even as Mom kneels on the ground and helps her put on her light-up shoes.

"Why doesn't Dani have to go?" she asks. Her voice is high pitched, like it usually is before a tantrum.

I watch from the living room sofa as Mom pulls Shelby's laces and begins tying them into a bow. "Dani and I are going to have a big girl talk with Daddy," Mom says. "You are going to have so much fun with Nana and Pop. I bet they'd love to see your Barbies."

Shelby stops sticking her lip out and gasps. "How many can I take?" she asks.

"As many as you want," Mom says.

Shelby leaps up and runs toward her bedroom. Mom sighs. "I might regret saying that," she says. She looks at me. "Will you be okay here until I drop her off?"

It's a ridiculous question, but I can't be rude to her two days in a row, so I only nod. I'm not really ready to speak—I feel weird, like if I open my mouth, I'll still be that mean girl who yells at her mom from yesterday.

Shelby comes back holding a medium-sized tote full of Barbies, their hair and arms sticking up out of the top.

"Ready!" she says. She doesn't say goodbye or look toward me.

Mom takes Shelby's hand, and they walk toward the front door. "See you in a few minutes," she calls over her shoulder.

Mom has barely made it back home when I hear the rumble of Dad's station wagon in the driveway. He comes in, and it seems odd to see him standing alongside Mom in the living room. I stare at both of them, but I don't get off the couch.

"Hey Dani," Dad says. He's wearing a wrinkled t-shirt, and I almost want to ask Mom to iron it for him. She used to wake up in the morning before anyone else and iron his dress shirts and slacks. I would sometimes wake up, warm in my bed, listening to the hiss of the iron through the wall.

"Hi," I say instead.

Mom claps her hands together. I can tell she's nervous because she keeps rocking back on her heels. She's smiling, but it's the same smile from Christmas when she told us we were going to Disney World. "Let's go into the kitchen and sit around the table, where it's more comfortable."

I want to tell her the hard kitchen chairs are not more comfortable than the sofa, but I stand up and follow.

In the kitchen, Dad sits, and I sit next to him. Mom pours Dad a glass of water, like he's a guest, not someone who used to live here with us and pour his own water. Then she sits, too. For a moment, we all just look down at the table, quiet.

"Your mom tells me you had a hard day yesterday," Dad starts.

I laugh a little but keep looking at the table. "You could say that. It stinks you weren't here."

Dad sighs and shifts in his seat. "I'm sorry about that, Dani. Work has been…" I can hear the noise of his hand rubbing against the stubble on his face as he pauses. "…insane. With all the technology stuff. You know what I'm talking about."

"Yeah," I say, finally looking up at him. He's now running his thumb along the edge of his cup. Mom keeps looking between the cup and me.

"But nothing happened," she says, then smiles. "With Y2K, I mean. Here we all are, safe and sound."

"Right," says Dad. "Everything worked out okay. At work and everywhere else." He pushes up his glasses and looks me in the eye, finally. "Are you, like, disappointed?"

"Disappointed?" I ask, even though I know what he means.

"Did you want everything to—I don't know— implode?" Dad asks. His cheeks are starting to get a little red, and for the first time, I notice wrinkles around his eyes. There are a few specks of gray in his rough beard. "Did you want the world to just fall apart?"

"No," I say, and I mean it.

"Then what's the deal?" Dad asks. His voice is getting louder, and Mom hisses, "*Kenny!*" and then mutters something else to him, but I can't make it out. I don't want to look at Dad right now, so I look at some dumb picture on the wall. It's a drawing of a chef's hat, and beneath it reads: "*So many recipes, so little thyme*" in curly cursive font. Mom thinks it's hilarious.

When I look back at Dad, he's taking a deep breath, and when he talks again, his voice is quieter. "Your mom tells me you cried all day. And then you were disrespectful to her. There's no excuse for that."

"I know," I say. "I really am sorry." I look at Mom, and she smiles at me. I feel forgiven.

"If you weren't disappointed, why did you get so upset?" Mom asks, leaning forward.

I shrug, but I can tell they both want an answer. My thoughts are in jumbles, like when Shelby tangled all her dress-up necklaces into a giant wad, and they wouldn't come apart. I try to sort them out. "I like to plan," I say, finally. "It feels good to not have any surprises. And when nothing happened on New Year's Eve, that felt like a surprise. A bad surprise, because I wasn't ready for it."

"But why do you have to plan so much?" Mom asks. "Do you feel nervous? Or insecure? You know we'll take care of you no matter what happens. Right?"

"I know that," I say. I can feel that tickling sensation in the back of my throat that means I'm about to cry, but I swallow it away. I need to say this. "But you guys have given me some bad surprises, too."

Mom and Dad look confused for a moment, but then I see understanding wash over their faces. I know they're remembering it just like I am: sitting inside the dark van, the boom of fireworks still ringing in our ears, my tongue still cold from popsicles, and our family falling apart. Or imploding, like Dad said.

"And after that, everything was different," I say. I suddenly feel like I'm running down the slope of a mountain, my feet moving faster and faster on their own, my body unable to stop. "Mom, you're not the same. You were always the person who held everything together, and now it feels like anything goes—which sounds like it would be fun, but it's not. Sometimes I think if Shelby shaved her head you would just look the other way. And Dad, you don't even have real plates. Or a bedframe for our bed. Or a place for your TV to sit. Not many places for me and Shelby to sit, really." I take a breath, then keep going. I can't really look at either of them, so my gaze is locked somewhere in the space between their shoulders. "And some weekends you're too busy to even see us. And the plan is that we're supposed to be at your apartment on the weekend." The tickling sensation is growing stronger, but I can't cry. I won't cry. "You have to follow the plan!" I say quickly, and I realize too late that I shouted it more than said it. I'm ready to apologize, certain I'll be in trouble again. But Mom and Dad don't look upset with me. Instead, they're looking at each other.

Once, Mom put an apple pie in the oven and accidently set the timer for too long. Smoke billowed out of the stove and filled the kitchen, and we had to open the windows and doors for fresh air. And now, it's quiet, so I try to picture the silence filling the kitchen like smoke. It's awkward and uncomfortable, and I can't stand it anymore, but there's no window or door to open that will make it better. I can only wait.

"Why can't we all be together?" I blurt instead. It sounds like something a baby would ask, and I almost expect Mom and Dad to laugh at me.

Mom looks away from Dad and takes a deep breath. "That's really complicated, Dani," she says. "I'm not sure it's something you will understand."

"That's not a good explanation," I say. I try not to sound less angry, but I hate it when they tell me I'm too young to get something, or I won't understand a situation until I'm older. I want to know now. I want to understand now.

Mom opens her mouth to say something else, but Dad interrupts.

"A lot of it has to do with me," he says. Mom blinks at him, and if the conversation wasn't so serious, it would be funny how much she looks like a surprised owl. "I was working a lot—I am working a lot. Too much, really. And your mom wanted me to prioritize you and Shelby and spend more time at home. And I didn't do it."

"But you can fix it, right?" I ask, leaning forward. The solution seems so easy.

"Dani," Mom says. She's looking at me now, and her eyes are teary. "Sometimes people change. They grow apart. I want you to know that your dad and I tried very hard to make it work. We never wanted this to happen."

Dad nods. "And we still respect each other. And we're both crazy about you and your sister. You know that, don't you?"

"Yes," I say, and it's the truth. I know it in the way Dad's face gets all relaxed and smiley on Friday afternoons when I walk out of school and get in his car. I know it in the way Mom gives me and Shelby giant bear hugs when we come back home on Sunday night. I know it in the way Dad watches the same princess movies with Shelby that we've all seen a thousand times. I know it in the way Mom keeps a box of Lucky Spangles in the cabinet for me, even on mornings when she makes pancakes or French toast.

I know it in the way they're both looking at me now, like I'm the most important person in the room. They're a team, and we're a team, even if it's not the kind of team I planned for.

"I miss us being in one place," I say.

"I miss that, too," Dad says. "But I think we can still make that happen. What if we planned something new? What if we all had dinner together on Friday evenings, maybe?"

Mom nods her head. "That would be great. Maybe we could even go somewhere special, like the mall." She winks at me, and I remember the memory I shared with her on Christmas Eve.

"Yeah," Dad says. "And I've been putting off going shopping for the apartment, but I will. Today. You girls need a proper bed. And I'll even get some dishes." He laughs, a little nervously. "Do you have any suggestions, Martha Stewart?"

"I like blue," I say.

"Blue it is," Dad says.

For a moment, we all just smile at one another. Sitting with both Mom and Dad, not worrying about the parent who is not there, makes me feel so relaxed, like my bones are made of rubber. I remember something else I want to say and, finally, I feel brave enough to say it.

"I know I'm not normal," I say. I watch Dad's mouth go from a smile to a straight line. "I know all my interests are weird. I know it was weird to worry so much about Y2K, and not like makeup or clothes or gymnastics."

"Gymnastics?" Mom wrinkles her nose, confused, but I keep talking.

"I'm going to try to be different," I say. "I'm going to try to be more normal, I guess. Keep the weird things I'm thinking about to myself."

Dad laughs, and, at first, I think he's relieved. It was his Christmas Eve request, after all. Then he says, "For me, it was Grease."

Now I'm confused. "Grease?"

"Not the country or the stuff you use to cook," Dad says. "The musical with John Travolta. I saw it in theaters when I was in high school. And I was just...obsessed. I couldn't stop thinking about it. I saw it three more times. I knew all the songs and most of the lines. I even tried to style my hair into a ducktail, like they wore in the movie. I wore a leather jacket and carried a comb. It was...an interesting time in my life."

I can't help it—I burst out laughing. The idea of my serious Dad wearing a leather jacket and trying to be cool makes me feel like my side is about to split open. I laugh so hard I have to lay my head down on the table.

When I finally look back up to catch my breath, Mom and Dad are laughing, too.

When my laughter has turned into quieter giggles, Mom says, "For me, it was turtles."

"Turtles?" I say, and I'm laughing all over again.

"Yes," Mom has to nearly shout over my laughter. "I *loved* turtles. I cut pictures of them out of magazines, and I had a turtle lunch box, even though I was probably too old to carry it. I said I wanted to be a turtle scientist when I grew up."

"I don't think that's a real job," Dad says, but he's smiling. That makes me laugh again.

"I don't think so, either," Mom says. "But, like I said, I loved them. I even found a turtle in the park and brought it home and kept it in a shoe box. It got loose and crawled under the couch, and it bit Pop when he tried to get it out."

I try to imagine slow, soft-spoken Pop laying on the ground, attempting to fish out an angry turtle beneath a couch. I laugh until my stomach hurts, and all I can do is smile.

"What we're saying, Dani," Dad says, after I calm down, "is that you get it honest. You're just like Mom and me. And you're perfect. We'd never want you to change."

Mom nods in agreement, and I feel light again, just like I felt when we went to Palm Mall after Career Day.

"I'm glad we talked," Mom says, reaching across the table to hold my hand. This time I let her. "Is there anything else you want to talk about? Any other worries you have?"

Now that I've worked things out with Mom and Dad, something new pushes forward in my brain. I groan when I remember what I'll have to deal with next. "Well, there is school tomorrow. I talked so much about—you know." I put my face in my hands. "Everyone is going to make fun of me."

"Why don't I call your counselor?" I hear Mom ask. "What's her name—Ms. Paige? She's so nice."

The thought of Ms. Paige's smiley face office makes me groan even louder. I pick my head up. "No. I'll be okay. I can handle it."

Mom doesn't look convinced, but Dad smiles.

"You're a brave girl, Dani," Dad says, squeezing my shoulder.

"Thanks," I say to him. "You're pretty great too, even if your hair used to be in something called a *ducktail*."

And then we're laughing again.

We're Back!

By: Professor Prepared (professorprepared.com)

Hello, friends.

It appears we have arrived in the year 2000 unscathed. This, perhaps, might lead some of you to think that I was uninformed and can no longer be trusted. That is understandable. In fact, the closer we got to midnight on December 31st, the more I began to doubt the event myself. And, when the catastrophe that we anticipated never came, I realized that it is not Y2K that we must prepare for. There is a different disaster on the horizon, just as large and debilitating as what we feared Y2K might be.

Stay safe, stay informed, stay prepared for the worst, and stay tuned for more information.

The Professor Prepared Store has now reopened!

Chapter Thirteen

January 3rd, 2000

3 Days After

At first, I think everyone has forgotten.

The day starts pretty normally. In English, Mrs. Michaels raises her eyebrow at me as I come in and take a seat but, thankfully, she doesn't say anything. In my journal, I write about the boots I got for Christmas and nothing more. In Science, we learn about the formation of stars, and I'm tempted to raise my hand and talk about the North Star—how you can use it for navigation purposes if a compass isn't available. But then I remember the 31st, and I stop myself. In PE, Mr. Morris asks us all to sit on the floor of the gym and watch a video about racquetball on the television cart. Everyone is so busy trying not to fall asleep that no one even notices me or remembers my warnings about Y2K. I eat lunch by myself in the library, as usual, but it doesn't feel lonely like it sometimes does. It feels safe and good to have a routine again, and I start to think that maybe everything is going to be okay.

And then I walk into Journalism.

"Look everyone, she survived," Trinity squeals. She's surrounded by three or four other students. They're standing near the door, like they've been waiting for me. Almost on cue, they all start clapping. "Bravo, Danielle," Trinity says above the applause. "I knew you could do it!"

"Knock it off," I say to the group. I squeeze past them into the classroom, not caring if my backpack jostles anyone. Out of the corner of my eye, I see that Trinity is right behind me.

"I guess you'll have to get to work on that project now," Trinity says. She stands in front of me as I sit my backpack beside my assigned seat. I notice she has on a new-looking purple butterfly sweater and a Tamagotchi clipped to her belt loop. Christmas presents, no doubt. I'm not surprised that Trinity got so many useless trinkets. "It's probably not going to be your best work."

The project. Oh no. There's a funny feeling in my neck and chest, like I've waded into the deep end of the pool and am trying desperately to turn around and head back to shallower water. I look toward the front of the room to make sure Mr. Dennis didn't overhear her, but he's nowhere to be seen.

"What do you want, Trinity?" I ask. I want to sound tough, but instead I just sound tired.

Trinity blinks, like she's surprised by the question. "I just wanted to congratulate you on your survival," she repeats. She stutters a little at the end, then she straightens her shoulders. She puts on the smile she wears for the news broadcast or when she talks to adults. "My party went well, by the way. Thanks for asking!"

A girl standing nearby giggles. "It was really fun," she says. She winks at Trinity before continuing. "You would have loved it, Dani."

Trinity keeps smirking at me, but thankfully Mr. Dennis rushes into the room before she can say anything else. He's looking down, dabbing at a stain on his polo shirt with a wet paper towel. He makes a waving motion with his hand without ever looking at us, but we all know that means we need to be in a seat. Trinity gives me one final clap, then turns on her heel and heads to her desk. I can see the back of Riley's head a few seats in front of me. I am surprised he didn't hear the applause and everything that Trinity said, but then I see he's leaning forward, reading. When one of his books is open, he's oblivious to everything. I once saw him nearly step in front of a car at parent pickup, focused only on the pages of the book in his hand.

"Welcome back," Mr. Dennis says, finally looking up. "I hope everyone had a great break. We're officially in the new millennium, and you know what that means."

For one terrifying moment, I'm scared he's going to make fun of me, too.

"You have four days to get your Me in the New Millennium projects polished and ready for our presentation on Friday," Mr. Dennis says, and my body sinks into my chair in relief. "And don't forget—you won't have much time to work on these tomorrow, because we'll be filming the morning news. So, you'll want to get as much completed as you can today. Any questions?"

There aren't any, so Mr. Dennis says, "All right. Scatter."

I start to get up, but Trinity slaps something on my desk as she passes by. She doesn't say anything or even stop, but I immediately know what she's showing me. It's a stack of glossy photographs. A pink sticky note on the top reads, "I thought you'd like to see these!" with a smiley face. Of course Trinity is the type of student who carries around pink sticky notes.

I should get up and start my project and completely ignore the photographs. The amount of work I have to do to complete the project and get a decent grade is a little overwhelming. But I want to see the pictures. I'm not even sure why. I peel off the sticky note and start with the photograph on the top.

It's a picture of Trinity and two other girls from our class. She's in the middle, and she has her arms slung around both of them. They're standing near a cake wrapped in caution tape—it looks sloppy. Mom could have made a better one.

I go to the next photograph.

In this one, Trinity is wearing a gas mask. Two adults—her parents, I guess—are standing behind her, their hands on her shoulders. They're wearing gas masks, too.

I roll my eyes and go to the next photograph.

It's a picture of Trinity and some other kids from school. Everyone is smiling or holding up peace signs. Trinity is wearing goggles, and I sigh out loud. Goggles are not a prepping item. Someone else has their arm wrapped in gauze like a mummy. So uninformed. I think about telling her how inaccurate all her decorations are, but then remember it doesn't matter anymore. So, I go on to the next picture.

And what I see makes me feel frozen. Stuck.

Another group shot, Trinity still in her stupid goggles, mummy arm still in the frame. But this time, there is another person with the group. He's smiling. He's wearing a green football shirt. Even though the pictures are a little dark, I can tell that he's holding a book in his hand.

Riley.

It reminds me of the moment I discovered that Natalie had a new best friend, except it stings even more. At least Natalie's new friend wasn't my enemy.

Automatically, I stand up from my desk and turn around, trying to spot the traitor. I see him next to the weather wall, applying more tape to the cloud.

"Dani," Mr. Dennis is suddenly beside my desk. "Do you have any questions about your project?" He's looking at the photographs in my hand, his eyebrows raised.

I still feel slow and heavy, so I just shake my head.

"Good," says Mr. Dennis. "Let's get to work, okay? You can look at pictures of your friends later."

I want to laugh, but instead I just nod. When Mr. Dennis moves away, I head toward the weather wall.

"I'm trying to restore your artwork," Riley says when I walk up to him. He smiles. I want to smile, too, because no one else remembers that it was me who drew the expressions on the sun and the cloud. But I don't smile. I can't.

"Thanks," I say. I decide to just get it over with, like ripping off a bandage. "How was Trinity's party?"

Riley winces, like I jabbed him hard in the side, but he doesn't stop what he's doing or look at me. He moves on to taping up the sun. "It was a little boring," he says, quietly, as though he doesn't want Trinity to hear and get her feelings hurt. "Honestly, I'm surprised she invited me. I was going to see if you wanted to go, too, but you weren't on IM, so…" his voice trails off.

Then we just stand next to one another, quiet. Riley stops taping.

"I didn't know it was Y2K themed," Riley says, finally looking at me. "That part was stupid, honestly. Not that Y2K stuff is stupid. Just…it's a stupid idea for a party." He scratches the back of his neck, something I'm beginning to learn is a nervous habit. "You're not, like, mad, are you?"

I am, but I know I have no right to be. He's telling the truth; I wasn't on instant messenger. I didn't see the point, because I thought I'd never see him again. And that made me really sad, even though I tried hard not to think about it.

"No," I lie. "Just wondering if you had a good break. That's all."

Riley smiles, and I notice his smile is bigger than the one in Trinity's photograph. "It was okay. I was honestly ready to come back to school." He puts down the tape and takes a big step back to admire his work. Then he freezes, like he's thinking, before he asks his next question. "How are you…holding up?"

Everyone at school has either ignored me or made fun of me. I realize Riley is the first person I've encountered today who treats me carefully, like I'm a finnicky house plant or a vase made out of fragile glass.

"I'm okay," I say, even though I'm not. The photographs hurt every time I think about them. New Year's Eve hurts every time I think about it, too. It feels like the last sore throat I had. I would feel completely normal and forget I was sick, and then every time I would try to swallow or talk, my throat would remind me.

I think Riley probably knows I'm lying, but he doesn't push me any further. "I'm glad you came over here," he says, looking from the weather wall to me. "I was going to see if you wanted to hang out this week."

My knee-jerk reaction is to tell him no, that I'm too busy, that soon the world will end and there's no point in building a friendship. And then I remember that's not true, and I'm all out of excuses.

"Hang out?" I say, trying to buy myself some time.

"Yeah," Riley says. There's a stray soccer ball on the floor near us for tomorrow's sports segment, and Riley starts to roll it around with the toe of his shoe. "You know the arcade, in the Palm Mall?"

I nod, even though I've never been inside. And, after my happy excursion with Mom and Dad and Shelby, I've tried to avoid the mall as much as I can. But I know what he's talking about. I've seen the arcade near Teen Queen Boutique, a pink clothing store that smells like body spray. Mom drags me there every few months for what she calls a "girl's shopping trip," which consists of her forcing me to try on things I hate and don't want. We both usually leave the store in a bad mood.

"Well, they've got a new pinball machine, and it's *Zombies of the Saguaro Desert* themed," he says. His face gets really excited—big eyes, goofy grin—like someone was handing him a million dollar check. "There are only a few in the US, so we really lucked out. Anyway, I went there last week but it was too crowded to play much since everyone was on winter break. Mom says she'll drop me off there again on Wednesday while my sister is at ballet practice. I thought maybe you'd want to come and check it out."

I wonder how entertaining it will be watching Riley hover over a zombie pinball machine. I can imagine him going into a trance, the way he gets with his books. But I feel cornered, and I don't know how to back out.

And I'm not even sure I want to back out.

"Yeah," I say. "That would be fun, actually." I think it might be a lie, but when Riley practically beams in response, I can't feel too bad about it.

Chapter Fourteen

January 4th, 2000

4 Days After

Mr. Dennis is a pretty laid-back teacher in a lot of ways, but he takes our morning news show very seriously. I think it's because he used to be a journalist himself. He wasn't on television, but he did work for a big newspaper. And on days when the news is filmed, he treats us more like employees than students.

It's always filmed on Tuesdays and broadcast on Wednesday mornings to the television carts in all the classrooms. It's not live, of course, but Mr. Dennis makes us act as though it is. Everyone has a job to do, and there's a grade penalty for messing up. There's an even bigger penalty if your mistake causes you to freeze or fall apart, and the segment has to be refilmed. Mr. Dennis says there's mistakes on air all the time; a good reporter or crew member will just carry on.

Jobs for morning news rotate every week, except for lead anchor, which is always Trinity. It isn't fair, and Mr. Dennis wasn't crazy about the idea, either. But Trinity argued that the consistency was good for the show.

"Look at Good Morning America, Mr. Dennis," Trinity said. "Do they have a new anchor every week?" She didn't give him time to respond. "No, it's always Diane Sawyer every morning." Most of the people in the class were too intimidated to argue, and no one else really wanted to be lead anchor, anyway, so Mr. Dennis just sighed and told her she could have the job.

I wish she were bad at it. But she's not. She actually does a good job reading off the copy in front of her and making eye contact with the camera. Everyone else, including me, just reads off the paper or looks at their feet when they have a reporting job. And Trinity enunciates and smiles in all the right places.

That's part of the reason I decide to sabotage her.

My job in this rotation is Prop Manager, which is one of the easier duties. I make a checklist and try not to think about another checklist I made just four short days ago. I ensure there is an umbrella near the weather wall since we had a brief, unexpected rain shower yesterday. *Check.* I find a couple of golf balls to add to the props for the sports segment. *Check.* I gather the copy for Trinity to read from, straighten it, and sit it on the news desk. *Check.*

My classmates are bustling all around me, trying to get cameras in the right spot and microphones plugged in. It's always chaotic, and the noise makes my head feel strange and buzzy. Someone shouts that one of the tripods keeps falling over. Someone else asks if anyone has seen Katie, who was assigned to the weather report this week. One of the microphones makes a loud, staticky noise. Katie shouts that she has returned from the restroom. Trinity is having another student braid her hair. We accidentally make eye contact, and she rolls her eyes at me. I can feel my cheeks heat up.

It's the eye roll that helps me make my decision. When I hear Trinity ask Mr. Dennis a question, I go back to the news desk and grab Trinity's papers. I pull a sheet from the middle of the stack and wad it into a ball, thankful the noise of commotion and talking and shuffling feet is loud enough to hide the sound of crinkling paper. I shove it in the kangaroo pocket of my hoodie. Then I place the papers back as neatly as they were before.

"Everything ready? Are we ready? Places, please," Mr. Dennis snaps his fingers and everyone hurries to their assigned spot. The room goes from a loud hum to completely silent, as it always does. Trinity practically skips behind the news desk and flips her newly braided hair behind her shoulders. I see Riley behind the camera, and I hear his clear voice counting down.

"3,2,1..."

The countdown reminds me of four days ago, too. I try to shake the memory away. I focus on Trinity, and my pain turns into excitement. It makes me feel a little like a villain in a movie, and I almost have to stop myself from twirling an imaginary moustache.

"We're rolling," Riley says. The light on his camera turns red.

"Good morning, Lowell Middle School," Trinity says, then smiles. She glances down for only a second. "Welcome to the first morning broadcast of the millennium. A new year means a fresh slate, so make sure you're ready to apply yourself and study hard, panthers! Now over to Katie for the weather report. Katie?"

The camera pivots toward the weather wall, and I am relieved when Katie is able to both talk and open the umbrella at the same time. I almost forget about stealing Trinity's script until the camera is back on her.

"Thanks, Katie, and stay dry, panthers!" Trinity glances down again. "Today for lunch we are having—" I hear the shuffle of paper. "—soccer tryouts."

Someone near me snorts out a laugh before they can stop themselves. Trinity's face changes from her confident newsworthy smile to complete panic—she's blinking, fast, and her mouth is a straight line. As for me, I'm smiling so wide my lips hurt. I probably look like an idiot, but it feels good. I feel victorious, the way I feel when I win over a particularly cranky townsperson in *Bounty Crescent*. Trinity clears her throat and tries again.

"Sorry about that, panthers," Trinity says, then gives a weak little laugh. "Today for lunch, we are actually having…" she shuffles through the entire paper stack, and I watch her face get paler. Her eyes are usually narrowed in a mean way, but now they're opening wider and wider. "It looks like I misplaced the menu, but I'm sure it's something both nutritious and yummy! Now on to Robbie for Sports!"

The camera shifts to Robbie and, as soon as it does, Trinity levels her gaze at me. She's angry, and her jaw is clenched tight. She mouths something I can't decipher.

But I just keep smiling.

At last, the camera returns to Trinity, who breathes deeply through her nose and resumes her own smiling just in time. "That's all for today. Have a good one, panthers!"

As soon as Riley yells, "Cut!" Trinity is out of her seat and pointing a finger at me. She's talking, though, to Mr. Dennis. "She messed up my script!" she screeches. She stomps toward me, stopping so close that we could stand toe to toe. I can see how hard she is breathing and the red splotches blooming on her cheeks.

"All right, Trinity, just calm down," Mr. Dennis says from his spot behind Riley.

But Trinity doesn't calm down or look away from me. "I don't want her actions to affect my grade," Trinity continues, like Mr. Dennis never even said anything. "I shouldn't be penalized because she's a miserable person and wants everyone else to be miserable, too." She's so close now that I see tears in her eyes—but that can't be right. It has to be the fluorescent lights in the classroom creating some sort of optical illusion.

"I have no idea what she's talking about," I say. I try to stand in such a way that the bulge in my hoodie pocket isn't visible. But I don't back down or move away from her. I'm not scared of her. I'm just *so* angry.

"Liar!" Trinity yells. Her bottom lip trembles, which surprises me, but I try not to let it show. "You did it to get back at me. I know you did!"

"You shouldn't be so paranoid, Trinity," I say. "You seem like a really gloomy person, honestly."

I see the recognition flash in Trinity's eyes, and she opens her mouth to say something else, but Mr. Dennis steps between us.

"All right, all right. I want half the class to work on putting up the props and equipment, the other half editing today's video. I'm going to call Ms. Paige and see if she can escort you both to her office before you disrupt my class any further."

Ms. Paige offers us bottled water, but we shake our heads. I choose the chair again. Trinity sits in the bean bag farthest from me.

Ms. Paige's office is so quiet—the only noise is the whir of the air conditioner. Ms. Paige taps a smiley face pen on her smiley face desk calendar. She smiles at both of us. I don't smile back. I can't see Trinity since she's sitting behind me, but I'm pretty sure she doesn't smile back, either.

"Sometimes, in stressful situations, our nerves can really get the best of us," Ms. Paige says in her calm, measured voice. "I can't imagine how stressful it must be to put a news broadcast together. That's a lot of pressure."

"That's not even it," I hear Trinity grumble.

"Do you care to expand on that, Trinity?" Mrs. Paige asks, craning her neck to look past me.

I can hear Trinity sigh, like Ms. Paige is too stupid to get it. I feel a flash of anger on Ms. Paige's behalf before Trinity finally speaks. "The news broadcast isn't stressful at all. That's not what happened. What happened was that *Danielle*—" she says my name like someone would say the word booger, "—messed up my copy, which caused me to mess up. Which never happens, Ms. Paige."

I make the laugh-scoffing noise that Trinity always brings out of me.

"Is that true, Dani?" Ms. Paige asks. Now she's looking straight at me. She isn't smiling. She looks serious.

"Yeah," I say. "I mean. I did take one of the pages."

I can hear Trinity gasp and shift on the bean bag behind me.

"But Trinity has been harassing me non-stop since we got back to school," I say. "You know, about the Y2K stuff." I say the last half more to my lap than to Ms. Paige.

"Is that true, Trinity?" Ms. Paige asks, gazing over my shoulder again. She's still not smiling.

"Yes," Trinity says. I refuse to turn around, but it sounds as though she's speaking mostly to the ground, too.

"Mr. Dennis says there's always been some animosity between you two," Ms. Paige says, gesturing between us. "Care to explain that to me?"

"She's just mad because the world didn't end like she wanted it to," Trinity says. "I don't know why she has to take it out on me."

I'm glad I didn't take Ms. Paige up on the water because hearing Trinity make that statement would have caused a tsunami-sized spit-take.

"You can't be serious," I say, finally turning around to look at her. Her arms are folded in front of her chest and her nose is turned upward, like a baby. Like Shelby. She looks ridiculous, especially surrounded by so many smiley faces. "*You* are always directing comments at *me*. Not the other way around."

"You don't even remember, do you?" Trinity asks. Her voice is quiet but rumbly. She's looking at me as though she wants to break Ms. Paige's smiley face coffee mug over my head.

"Remember what?" I ask.

Trinity groans and reclines back on her hands. The beanbag makes a crunchy noise beneath her. "Nevermind. Forget it. Ms. Paige, can I please go back to class?" She stretches out the word *please*.

I turn back to Ms. Paige, who is studying Trinity with a serious expression on her face. She sighs, and finally reaches for her pad of yellow hall passes. "Yes, you may," Ms. Paige begins. "But just so you know, I'll be calling you back down here in a few minutes so you can explain your earlier comment, understood?" She pauses to get some sort of confirmation from Trinity. I can't see Trinity's face, but she must have said the right thing, because Ms. Paige rips out the hall pass and holds it between her thumb and pointer finger. "Dani, can you stick around for a minute? I want to talk to you in private."

Trinity stands, takes the hall pass, and smiles down at me, like she won a contest between the two of us. I struggle to keep my face blank. When the door closes behind Trinity, Ms. Paige smiles at me once again.

"You know," she says. "I feel partly responsible for all of this."

My eyebrows raise in confusion.

"I spoke to your mother, and I meant to call you down to my office first thing yesterday morning, but then I was swamped with all these scheduling changes." She gestures to the large box-like computer on her desk, as though I can see all the scheduling changes inside of it. "I'm really sorry. I should have checked in with you sooner and maybe we could have diffused this whole thing."

I don't know what to say. It's weird to hear an adult taking the blame for something I did, apologizing to *me*. I settle for, "That's okay."

"How are you feeling?" Ms. Paige asks. She puts her elbows on the table and leans forward a little, looking me in the eye. And I realize Riley might not be the only person at school who treats me like I might break—like I might *matter*.

I want to tell her I'm fine, but Ms. Paige knows me pretty well at this point. "I'm embarrassed," I say. I rub my hand across my face. I just keep thinking about these Russian nesting dolls Nana keeps in one of her curio cabinets. I'd like to do that—go inside myself over and over again, until I'm completely protected and safe.

Ms. Paige nods. Then she steeples her fingers. "Can I share something with you, Dani? I want this to stay between us. Can I trust you to do that? Since we're kindred spirits and all?"

I sit up a bit straighter. "Sure," I say. "Of course."

"I thought so," Ms. Paige says. "I have a story for you. I went to a family reunion last summer. There were so many people there. I hadn't seen some of them in years, and I wanted to look nice, so I wore a dress. The reunion was at a park, and they only had these really small, dirty public restrooms." Ms. Paige wrinkles her nose at the memory. "So, it's almost time to eat—they were grilling kosher dogs and other yummy stuff—and I decided to run to the restroom. I tried to be really fast because the bathrooms were so gross. I washed my hands, came back out, and got in line to grab some food. I'm talking to the people in front of me and laughing and having a great time."

Ms. Paige is cool and all, but like all adults, she can really ramble. I blink, waiting for the point. I don't wait for long.

"The whole time," Ms. Paige says, leaning forward and talking in a near whisper, "my dress was tucked into my panty hose. In the back. So, everyone behind me— well, they got a show." She blushes, and it's an expression I've never seen from her before.

A laugh bursts out of me, but I quickly clamp my hand over my mouth.

"When someone finally came up and told me, I was mortified," Ms. Paige says. "I wanted to leave and never come back. But I knew I would have to see some of those people in a few months for Chanukah. I didn't know how I was going to handle it."

"How did you handle it?" I ask.

"I read a lot about embarrassment," Ms. Paige says. "There's a lot of really interesting research about the best way to handle embarrassing situations, and there's a lot of science behind why we feel embarrassment in the first place. I won't bore you with all of that, though. What it boiled down to was this: The best way to handle embarrassment is with a sense of humor. So, when it was time to see some of those people again, I walked in and said, 'Sorry to disappoint, but I decided to go with pants this time!' Everyone laughed, and then no one brought it up again." Ms. Paige begins writing a second hall pass for me, but she doesn't stop speaking. "Embarrassment stings, Dani. I know. And I don't know when it will happen for you, but I promise that, at some point, you will be able to laugh about it."

"And until then?" I ask.

Ms. Paige hands me the hall pass and gives me one of her big smiles. And unlike the smiley faces on her rug and posters and paper clips, this smile feels genuine and warm. "Until then, my door is always open."

It's hard not to think about Trinity that evening when I'm outside Nana and Pop's house scooping up rotten fruit. Mom dropped me off so I could help pick up around their lawn, part of my punishment for my bad behavior right before Christmas. "Look at all these oranges and lemons," Mom said in the car, gesturing to the fruit that was once in Nana and Pop's trees and was now brown and mushy on the ground. "I expect all of it to be gone when I come back. Understood?"

I'm replaying Trinity's comment—*you don't even remember, do you?* —and putting a particularly squishy orange into a garbage bag when I can hear the steady plodding noise of Pop's cane.

"Nice of you to help us out," Pop says suddenly from beside me. "Most kids your age would be too busy running around with their buddies to lend a hand."

I realize Mom must not have mentioned that my volunteering was punishment, so I decide not to mention it, either.

"Well," I say, bending to pick up a lemon. "I don't have a ton of friends."

Pop waves me away with one wrinkled hand. "I know that's a load of crock. Smart girl like you has a lot to offer." He taps his walking stick on the brown grass. "You're like your mother. She was pretty shy, too. But she was more comfortable having a few good friends as opposed to a big group of friends. Nothing wrong with that."

Pop hobbles a little closer to squeeze my shoulder, and then I hear the creak of the door as he goes back into the house. Something about his words makes me remember Riley's kind eyes, and his zombie books, and his quick, happy responses on IM.

When Mom comes to get me an hour later, I've made up my mind. I want to go to the arcade.

A New Catastrophe Approaches

By: Professor Prepared (professorprepared.com)

As you can probably guess, I've received many emails and entries to my guest book in the last few days. Some readers are curious about the looming disaster I described in my last blog post. Others are asking for refunds for items they purchased from the Professor Prepared store.

Friends, I urge you to hold on to your supplies and stay vigilant. Due, in large part, to the warnings of informed preppers like me, January 1st, 2000, caused no major problems around the globe. There is an upcoming date, however, that I believe computer scientists have not yet planned for.

February 29th, 2000. That's right, readers. The year 2000 contains a Leap Day, and this quirk on top of the change from 1999 to 2000 will surely boggle our computers' electronic brains. I urge you to do some research on the matter and, until then, hold tight to your supplies and continue to check this website for further information.

Stay safe, stay informed, and prepare for the worst. Good luck to you.

Want to be ready for Leap Day 2K? We have everything you need in the Professor Prepared Store!

Chapter Fifteen

January 5th, 2000

5 Days After

Alone in my bedroom, I decide to change out of my school clothes. I swap my long-sleeved shirt for the succulent hoodie Dad bought me for Christmas. I give my vanity mirror one short, passing glance. My stomach feels fluttery, like it sometimes does when I have to give a presentation in class. I try not to look in the direction of my shelves or even go near them. I used to spend hours in that exact spot, organizing and stacking. When the 31st drew closer, I spent a lot of time just staring at everything, straightening the cans so the labels faced the same way or organizing the water containers from most to least full. I used to look at the shelves and feel so proud—smart and grown up and sensible. Now I look at the shelves and feel foolish.

In the living room, Mom is sitting on the floor with Shelby, reading a book. Mom bought that silly divorce workbook for me, but for Shelby she bought a huge stack of children's books. They're still about divorce, but the families are opossums or unicorns or bees in a hive and not people. Mom gives one of the characters a deep, rumbling voice. Shelby laughs and burrows her head into Mom's shoulder. I watch them for a minute, dreading the moment when I have to interrupt.

Thankfully, Mom notices me first. She closes the book. "Everything okay, Dani?"

I nod. "Yeah, everything's great. I was just…" I push my sleeves up and then pull them back down. "I was just wondering if you could give me a ride."

Shelby grabs the book from Mom's hands and starts pawing through it herself.

"Give you a ride where?" Mom asks.

"To the arcade," I say. "My friend, Riley, asked me to drop by."

I see Mom's eyes change—they look wider and brighter. "Riley?" she says. "You've never told me about anyone named Riley." A part of me hopes she's saying no, but she slowly stands up from the carpet. "This is good, Dani. When Natalie moved away, I thought…" Whatever she was going to say, she doesn't finish it. "Of course I'll take you. What do you say, Shelby? You want to go on a ride?"

"Can we get ice cream?" Shelby asks, dropping the book like it's on fire.

"We could probably do that," Mom says. Shelby cheers and runs to get her shoes.

Half an hour later, Mom parks near the Palm Mall. I can remember it opening when I was around Shelby's age. The building used to be bright yellow; now the sun has dulled it to a pale butter color. There are big palm tree-shaped neon signs near the entrance, but they're rusty and never turned on.

"Get out so we can get ice cream," Shelby says from her booster seat.

"Shelby," Mom scolds. She turns to me. "We'll be back in an hour or so to pick you up. I'll park here. Okay?"

"You can come back sooner, if you want," I say. "I doubt I'll even want to stay that long."

Mom huffs. "Try to have a little fun, Dani, okay?"

I climb out of the van and walk toward the mall. My stomach feels super fluttery now, like it did the one time I rode a roller coaster with loops and swore to never get on another one. When I open the black glass doors of Palm Mall, I'm first greeted by the smells and noise of the food court. I walk past the square tables, past a kiosk selling earrings. I cough as I pass Teen Queen Boutique and get a whiff of body spray, and then I hear the beeping of the arcade.

Inside, it's a little dark, and the carpets have a crazy zigzag pattern that glows. There's a little kid and her dad playing skee ball. The kid isn't very good; most of her balls are landing on the floor. An older teenager is bent toward a machine, his mouth hanging open. I peer over his shoulder at the screen, and I can see two guys in ninja outfits kicking each other over and over again. Moving deeper inside, I find a row of pinball machines. Only one person is playing them, so I spot the back of Riley's head right away.

For a moment, I just watch him. It feels a little weird because he doesn't know I'm there, but what I see is kind of surprising, too. At school, Riley is composed. His voice is quiet; his movements are slow. Bent over the pinball machine, Riley isn't saying anything, but his hands are moving lightning fast over the various silver knobs. He dances from foot and foot. Something upsetting must happen, because he groans and punches the air.

I decide this is as good a time as any. I tap him on the shoulder. He spins around, and smiles when he sees that it's me.

"Hey!" he says. "You made it!"

I nod. "So, this is it?" I ask, gesturing toward the pinball machine.

"It is!" Riley knocks gently on the glass. It reminds me of the way my uncle always knocks on the hood of the sports car he's particularly proud of. Riley points to all the various characters painted on the machine and tells me all their names. In each portrayal, the character is either running from a zombie, swinging a weapon at a zombie's rotting face, or looking toward the player with a tough expression. I smile and listen and try to act interested.

"Honestly, I didn't know if you would come," Riley says suddenly. "After, you know, all that stuff with Trinity yesterday."

"That wasn't a big deal," I say. "I'm fine."

It was a big deal; just the sight of Trinity today at school made me so angry that my stomach hurt. But Ms. Paige and Mr. Dennis said if we kept our distance from one another, our parents wouldn't be contacted about our spat. I spent the school day staying out of her way, and she seemed determined to stay out of mine. I even kept my face neutral when Ms. Paige called her down to the guidance office during Journalism, but I did notice she returned looking a little teary.

"Trinity can be really mean," Riley says. He reaches toward the pinball machine and starts a new game. "She cares way too much about what other people think of her," he continues over his shoulder.

I step closer so I can watch him play. The lights of the machine blink on and off. Sometimes, a bell rings or a quiet alarm sounds. Sometimes a muffled voice comes out of the tiny speakers. I don't understand any of it.

"That's true," I say. "You've figured her out, and you haven't even known her very long. My mom would say that makes you a good judge of character."

Riley looks pleased at that, and puffs his chest out a little. "I'd like to think so," he says. The machine makes a growling sound effect—a zombie, I guess—and the lights flash red. "Aw man," Riley says. "Game over."

"Sorry," I say.

"Do you want to play?" Riley asks.

It feels kind of like an honor—Riley sharing his beloved pinball machine with me. But I shake my head. "I'd rather watch you," I say.

Riley returns his hands to the knobs, and I watch as a spring shoots a silver metal ball in an arc. The ball tunnels its way past lights and images before being flipped by a paddle into a new path.

"I feel like maybe I've figured you out, too," Riley says.

I look from the glass of the machine to his face, surprised. "Oh yeah?" I say, because I can't think of anything else to fill the silence.

"Yeah," he says. "Remember that character I said reminded me of you? Joan?" The machine growls again, and Riley doesn't complain about his loss this time.

Instead, he points to a girl painted on the machine. She has long blonde hair past her waist, and she's hefting a bloody ax in her muscled arms. She's beautiful.

"She doesn't look anything like me," I say, embarrassed.

It's hard to tell because the lighting is so dim in the arcade, but Riley looks like he blushes a little. "It's not that so much," Riley says. "It's her personality, mostly."

"Is she weird, too?" I ask. I laugh, but really, I'm hoping she's not weird at all.

Riley shakes his head. "She's absolutely not weird," he says. I feel my shoulders slump in relief. The machine goes dark, probably because Riley hasn't touched it since he lost. I expect Riley to reach for it again, but instead he says, "Want to get a smoothie?"

We leave the arcade and wind our way through the food court, stopping at Smoothie Shack. I use my Christmas money and choose a pineapple flavor; Riley gets mango. We find a bench across from Best Buddy Factory. Inside the store, we can see kids about Shelby's age choosing deflated stuffed animals and filling them up with white cottony fluff. A little girl cries when the ballerina shoes she selected for her stuffed horse don't fit on its hooved feet. I start to comment on that, but Riley speaks first.

"So, Joan," he says, like the conversation in the arcade never stopped. "She's the youngest of the group. In the first book, anyway. And, when she first finds the other survivors, everyone wants to ditch her. It's like, you only need useful people during the apocalypse, you know?" I want to tell Riley I can't be like Joan, then, because I *am* useful, but I decide to let him continue. He stops to take a slurp of his smoothie before he speaks again. "And they think she's dead weight. She's little, and she's another mouth to feed. But pretty soon they learn that Joan's greatest abilities don't have anything to do with her physical strength."

Riley takes a breath. The cashier put a little umbrella in my drink, and I drag it through the slush and try not to look too interested.

"She came from a survivalist background. She knows how to can food and how to find water and how to orient the group when they get lost in the woods. She knows how to start fires. She knows the edible plants from the poisonous ones. But, as time passes, she becomes the *most* useful person in the group. Even more important than the good fighters."

Something in my chest feels light and fluttery—it's the roller coaster feeling again. "She sounds cool," I say, and try to keep my voice steady.

"She really is," Riley says. "And, you know, after the zombie uprising, no one uses their real name anymore. Everyone takes on a new persona. Some people get real creative—there's one dude that goes by Hephaestus. So, Joan, her real name is Brittany or Ashley, something normal. But she chooses to go by Joan after Joan of Arc. You know, the hero?"

I conjure up a foggy memory of a crumbling French statue in one of my history books. "Oh yeah," I say.

"Joan of Arc said this quote—well, people say she said it. Historians don't really know. It's a cool saying, though. It goes, 'I am not afraid. I was born to do this.'" Riley pauses to take another drink. "In the books, Joan says that all the time. It's like the code she lives by." In a lower, quieter voice, Riley adds, "And that quote always makes me think of you."

I suddenly feel brave, like I could take on a hoard of zombies myself. "Why?" I ask.

"Because you weren't interested in the Y2K stuff because you were afraid. You liked being ready for anything." Riley sits his cup on the ground and looks at me. He doesn't make eye contact much, so his gaze makes me feel sort of squirmy. "I know sometimes you feel different because of all the things you know. You feel like no one else gets it. But you shouldn't be ashamed. It's your greatest strength. You were born to be prepared, to keep people safe. Like Joan."

Riley's words stir something in me, and suddenly I'm remembering what Ms. Paige said, too.

I am not afraid. I was born to do this. At some point, you will be able to laugh about it.

"Riley," I say. "I have an idea for my Me in the New Millennium project, I think. But I'm going to need your help tomorrow. I'm super behind."

Riley smiles. "I thought you'd never ask," he says.

We finish our smoothies and walk back to the arcade. I even take a shot at playing pinball, though I lose almost immediately. Nearly two hours have passed when we say our goodbyes, and I head back out to the parking lot and find Mom's van.

Shelby is asleep in her booster seat, her head tilted back and her mouth wide open. Her face looks sticky, probably from ice cream. Mom is reading a magazine positioned over her steering wheel.

"Sorry that took so long," I say, sliding the van door closed behind me.

Mom waves my apology away. "Did you have fun with Riley?" she asks.

I smile. "A lot of fun," I say. And this time, I'm telling the truth.

Chapter Sixteen

January 6th, 2000

6 Days After

Riley and I don't waste any time in Journalism class. Mr. Dennis has barely said "scatter" when he grabs a newly charged video camera, and we head out to the hallway to film.

"Do you know what you're going to say?" he asks.

I wave my hand around to indicate that I only *sort of* have a plan. I've written down a few rough notes in my sketchbook, and I sit it on the ground beside me. "Honestly, I'm a little overwhelmed," I say.

"Don't be," Riley says. "If we don't finish it up today, come over to my house after school. My dad has a video camera we can borrow."

I can't help it—I let out a huge breath. I feel so relieved I could melt into a puddle on the hard hallway floor. "Thank you, Riley."

He shrugs, like it's no big deal. But it is a big deal. I am likely losing major points after sabotaging our morning broadcast. This video, this project, has to be perfect if I have any hope of saving my Journalism grade.

"Let's just do a test run for now," Riley says. "Stand over there, and I'll work on framing the shot."

I stand against the cinderblock wall while Riley twists the camera onto a tripod. Then I see him fiddle with the buttons that zoom in and out, and the camera makes a churning noise. Finally, he squints into the viewfinder.

"Okay, say something," he says.

"Something," I say.

Riley and I both laugh.

Then we jump, because someone screams. Loud.

Riley pulls his face away from the video camera. His eyes are wide, and he's paler than usual. "What was that?" he asks.

I shake my head. Then we hear the scream again. The noise is so chilling the back of my head tingles. The sleeves of my button-down are pushed up, and I notice there's goosebumps on my forearms.

"That's coming from the classroom," Riley says, nodding toward Mr. Dennis's doorframe.

We run back toward the classroom door, abandoning our video camera. When we burst inside, we see our classmates gathered together at the front of the classroom, near the whiteboard. They're standing in a semicircle around something. No, *someone*. Someone on the ground.

It's Trinity.

Trinity is sitting on the floor, rocking back and forth on her bottom, and Mr. Dennis is standing beside her, nervously running his fingers down his necktie. Trinity's face is all screwed up, and her cheeks are wet with tears. She holds her right wrist with her left hand, and she clutches it to herself protectively. She screams again, and some of the students nearest her cover their ears.

Mr. Dennis looks as pale as Riley did in the hallway. "Trinity, you're going to have to stop screaming and tell me what happened." He keeps looking around the room, as if searching for the object or person who hurt his student.

"I was—" she stops and snuffles. Her nose is starting to run toward her lip. It's gross, and I know she must really be upset, because there's no way she'd normally let everyone see her like this. "I was doing a back hand-spring for...for the v-video. And w-when I flipped back, I f-fell." She bursts into loud sobs.

"I was filming her, Mr. Dennis," one of our class-mates pipes up. He's still holding a video camera, though it's off now. "I think she hurt her wrist."

I remember how Trinity bragged that she always got her hands in the correct spot while doing a back hand-spring. Part of me wants to laugh at the irony of the scene before me, but a bigger part of me is really scared by how loudly Trinity is crying.

"I told you, you have to be safe while doing that kind of stuff in here!" Mr. Dennis's face is red, but Trinity doesn't respond. She just keeps crying. Mr. Dennis scans the crowd of students standing around him.

"I can go get Nurse Collins," one of the boys volunteers.

Mr. Dennis shakes his head. When he speaks, it's like he's talking more to himself than to us. "Nurse Collins won't leave her exam room for anything less than an emergency. I'll go so I can stress how...*vocal* Trinity is being." He winces as Trinity cries out again. "All of you keep an eye on her until I get back."

He races out of the room, and then it's completely silent except for Trinity's whines and sniffling. For a few seconds, it's really awkward. Everyone is standing around, unsure of what to do, trying not to look at Trinity. Eventually, there's some quiet mutters of conversation. I hear people talking about their projects or what they're doing after school or the baseball game tomorrow night. Like there isn't a crying, injured girl on the floor.

But I can't ignore her. My eyes are locked on Trinity and her wrist.

Slowly, I approach her, like I would a wounded animal. When she notices, she angles her body away from me, as though she thinks I'm going to hurt her even more. "Get back," she says in a hiss. It's the first time she's stopped crying or screaming.

The conversation in the classroom quiets. Everyone is watching, and I know what they're thinking. They witnessed our fight, after all. They think I might hurt Trinity, too.

"Dani," Riley says from somewhere behind me. I can hear the worry in his voice, but I don't turn toward him. I keep inching forward, toward Trinity. I squat until I'm eye level with her wrist. "It doesn't look swollen," I say.

"So?" Trinity says. I think she wants to sound angry or tough, but her voice chokes with sobs again. "It really hurts," she says, and it sounds weaker than any tone I've ever heard Trinity use.

"I can tell," I say. "It's probably a really bad sprain." I carefully reach my hand toward her wrist. She recoils, and it reminds me of the time Shelby got a splinter in her finger but didn't want anyone to pinch it out. Finally, Trinity loosens her shoulders and extends her injured wrist to me. I circle it, gently, with my thumb and pointer finger, and slowly nudge her arm upward, toward her head.

"If it's sprained," I say, "you need to keep it elevated. Higher than your heart."

"Oh," Trinity says in a quiet voice. She uses her good hand to wipe her face with the collar of her shirt. "Thanks."

The conversation resumes around us, a little louder. Everyone sounds almost relieved.

"Where did you learn this?" Trinity asks. Her eyes are red and her face is blotchy, but she isn't crying anymore.

"Professor Prepared," I say. I can feel my cheeks heat up a little. "There was a post about first aid. About sprains and broken bones." I even practiced tying a tourniquet on one of Shelby's old dolls and practiced giving myself the Heimlich Maneuver. It feels like a lifetime ago.

"Figures," Trinity says, but she doesn't sound as mean as she normally does. I'm still holding her wrist upwards, and she's letting me. "What is taking Mr. Dennis so long?"

"I don't know," I say.

Trinity scoffs and looks down at the floor. For a moment, there is no conversation between us. There is only the talking of everyone else in the class. Someone even has the nerve to laugh out loud.

"I started thinking," Trinity says. She sniffles, and for a moment I'm scared she's going to start crying again, but she doesn't.

"About what?" I ask. My arm is getting tired holding her arm up, but I don't dare drop it.

"When we were in Ms. Paige's office, I realized you don't remember what happened in third grade. And then, when I went back to talk to Ms. Paige, she told me she thought you probably forgot, too. What you said to me. Do you remember?" She isn't asking in an angry way, just a curious way. I rack my brain trying to remember anything of significance from my third grade year. I have memories of rough Red Rover games on the playground, of Mom's swollen belly, and then baby Shelby coming home in a soft pink blanket. Trinity was in my class and annoying, as always, but I can't remember anything specific about her.

"No," I say. "Sorry."

Trinity shrugs. "It's dumb, I guess," she says. She sighs, deep, and her wrist bobs a little. "It was about my widow's peak." With her free hand, she points to her forehead, where her red hair dips into a slight vee. "Does that ring any bells?"

I shake my head and Trinity snorts.

"I didn't think so." Trinity takes a deep breath. "I can remember we were on the alphabet carpet. It was almost time to go home—we were waiting for the busses, I think. And you poked me on the forehead," she pokes her own forehead in demonstration, "and told everyone I had a widow's peak."

"Well," I said. "You do."

"Right," Trinity says. "But you didn't stop there. You told everyone that, according to legend, people who had widow's peaks were destined to become widows or widowers. Their husbands or wives would die. They were bad luck. You have always been full of weird facts like that." Trinity's eyes drift back to her injured wrist, still being held aloft in my hand. "No offense," she adds.

"I know," I say, and shrug as well as I can with one arm in the air. "None taken."

"Anyway, for months, everyone kept reminding me I was bad luck. No one would use the monkey bars after I touched them. I ate lunch all by myself. Somehow everything got so twisted that people were saying I was a witch. And not a cool witch, like Sabrina or Hermione Granger. The kind of witch that casts evil spells. I cried every morning before school. Once, I even held a thermometer to the light bulb in my bedroom so my mom would believe I was sick and let me stay home." Trinity's eyes look a little glassy at the memory. "All because of a stupid widow's peak."

I sit quietly for a moment, though my eyes find Riley. He's standing a few feet away, still watching me nervously. I should smile at him or mouth something, but instead I allow Trinity's words to wash over me like the rain showers we have during monsoon season. I've never had many friends, but I like being by myself, having quiet time to think and rest. I don't know if Pop was right about Mom, but he was definitely right about me. A few close friends—as opposed to a smorgasbord—makes me happiest. Trinity is different, though. In her world, acceptance is everything. Popularity is of the utmost importance. She wants to be surrounded by people, whether it's in class or at her own party. I can't imagine how painful third grade was for her. She'd probably prefer the sprained wrist over that pain again.

"I'm sorry," I say, and I mean it with my whole heart.

I feel Trinity's arm tremble a little. "It's okay," she says. She looks at me, and I notice one of her butterfly clips has come loose. Between the wild hair and the snot and the tears, I've never seen Trinity look like this. It makes me think that when she's at home, with her family, she's really just like me. "I mean, I accept your apology. And I'm sorry too. About everything."

"Thank you," I say, because I'm not sure what you say after someone apologizes to you after you apologize to them. My own arm is starting to feel a little numb and tingly. I'm about to tell Trinity I can no longer hold her wrist when Nurse Collins finally bustles into the room, Mr. Dennis on her heels.

"Clear out, everyone," Nurse Collins says in her deep voice, and all the students move away from Trinity and me. "Even you," she then adds, pointing at me. I let go of Trinity's wrist, but Trinity continues to hold it up high, even without my support. As I get to my feet, she smiles at me, and I know it is a thank you.

We all watch as Nurse Collins shuffles Trinity out of the room. When the classroom door shuts behind the two of them, Mr. Dennis turns back to us. His tie is flipped over his shoulder as though he were running a marathon. He's still breathing hard. "Excitement's over," he says between breaths. "Time to get back to work. Let's scatter."

I glance over at Riley, who is still standing in the same spot. He beams at me, the smile he uses when he talks about *Zombies of the Saguaro Desert.* I wonder what he's thinking—if taking care of Trinity reminded him of something Joan would do.

I walk to him and nudge his shoulder. "Come on," I say. "Let's get back to work."

Answering Your Questions

By: Professor Prepared (professorprepared.com)

As mentioned in my last update, I have been inundated with emails from readers of *Professor Prepared*. I have selected a few to share with all of you, along with my response.

Q: Hello, Professor Prepared. I work in technology for a large corporation. In preparing for the Y2K "disaster," my team and I also ensured that our computer systems would be able to work correctly on the upcoming Leap Day. All knowledgeable technology departments around the globe likely did the same. You are spreading fear and misinformation. It's probably time to pack it up. Sincerely, Frank S., Louisville, Kentucky.

A: Frank, thank you for your email. I am so glad that your reading of the Professor Prepared website enabled you to prevent your corporation from suffering any sort of complications on January 1st, 2000. Although I am glad to hear you feel confident in your abilities to navigate the upcoming Leap Day 2K, please know your experience is not universal. Good luck to you.

Q: Dear Professor Prepared—thank you sincerely for the heads up regarding the Leap Day 2K. In your opinion, what is the most essential item one will need to survive this looming catastrophe? Regards, Lionel B., Albuquerque, New Mexico.

A. A fantastic question, Lionel. Your e-mail definitely identified you as a true prepper. In many ways, Leap Day 2K will be exactly as we feared Y2K would be. Hopefully you stocked up on the essentials ahead of the 31st—canned food and bottled water, first aid kits, cash, batteries, etc. If I could make a suggestion for additional purposes, I would advise stocking up on weather-resistant gear as many areas are experiencing record low temps and surprise rain showers. Luckily for you, the Professor Prepared Store has recently added hooded sweatshirts, windbreakers, and stylish umbrellas. *Check them out here.*

Q: Dear Professor Prepared—based on your advice, I quit my job, sold a great deal of my belongings, and purchased a one-bedroom house deep in the woods. Imagine my surprise when the world was still standing after midnight on January 1st. Do you have any advice on how

I might go about reapplying for my old job? Also, how do you sleep at night? Yours, Rachel J., Raleigh, North Carolina.

A: Thanks for writing, Rachel. Surely your former place of employment knows that being prepared for emergencies is an important and necessary skill. I am sure they will welcome you back with open arms, though you might want to wait until February 29th is safely behind us before you actually return. I typically sleep in my bunker, lulled into dreamland by the sounds of my electric generator. Thanks again for your correspondence.

Q: Do you think I was born yesterday? Sincerely, Tom, Boston, Massachusetts.

A: No, Tom. I believe you are likely old enough to operate a computer, or else I wouldn't have received this email. I detect some sarcasm, so allow me to assure you I am not out to trick anyone. I am simply sharing the information I have in hopes it will compel others to plan accordingly. Good luck to you, sir.

Want to send an email to Professor Prepared? Do so in style with our limited edition Professor Prepared mouse pad. Now available in the Professor Prepared Store!

Chapter Seventeen

January 7th, 2000

7 Days After

Soft flute music plays on the television cart at the front of the classroom. Onscreen, there is a photo slideshow—Trinity as a child, walking across a balance beam in a pink leotard. Trinity doing some sort of flip, her hands and feet blurred in motion. A recent photo of Trinity holding a shiny trophy. Another recent shot of her clutching a bouquet of roses.

Sitting at my desk, I hope we are watching the final seconds of Trinity's Me in the New Millennium project, though I try not to let that show on my face. Mostly because Trinity and I are good now, but also because she is standing only feet away, beside the television cart, her arm in a sling. I had to stop myself from rolling my eyes when I saw she had decorated the straps with holographic butterfly stickers. "Thank you, everyone, for your help and concern," Trinity said upon entering Journalism class. "Dani was correct—my wrist is indeed sprained. But I'm prepared to continue anchoring the morning news." She stared at the entire class until we offered a quiet, half-hearted applause.

Now, on the television, there is a short roll of credits—*Starring Trinity Taylor, Directed by Trinity Taylor*—and then my classmates give the same slow, unenthusiastic claps. But Trinity beams like this is her Oscars award ceremony. "Thanks, everyone!" she says, then sits back down at her desk.

Mr. Dennis smiles from behind his own desk, but his eyes look sleepy. "Thank you, Trinity," he says. "I appreciate you volunteering to go first, as always." He spins a little in his chair so he can see us all. "Any other volunteers?"

No one moves. So, I lift my hand, slowly, into the air, even though my heart feels like a hummingbird in my chest.

"Dani?" Mr. Dennis seems a little surprised, but he shrugs and gestures toward the television cart. "Go ahead."

I stand, and my legs feel a bit wobbly, but I head to the front of the classroom and slip the tiny cassette into the video camera on the cart. It's hooked via red and yellow wires to the television, which makes it look intimidating and robotic. Or maybe it's just my nervous brain playing tricks on me. Despite working on my project for hours after school at Riley's house, despite watching it myself several times, I still don't feel fully confident in what Mr. Dennis and my classmates are about to see.

But I take a deep breath. And I make my hand press play.

Onscreen, there is the beginnings of a black and white cartoon. It took some serious digging on the internet, and twice we had to disconnect because Riley's

Mom needed to use the phone, but we finally found the cartoon Nana talked about in her canning room during our Christmas visit—*Duck and Cover*. A turtle moseys down the street wearing a helmet. A monkey suddenly appears from within a tree, dangling a stick of dynamite in front of his surprised face. The turtle disappears inside its shell just before the stick of dynamite explodes, leaving only remnants of the charred black tree and a safe, intact turtle.

And, thanks to Riley's editing skills, the next shot is me, in black and white, standing in his living room. I am ducking, covering my head in much the same way the turtle was covered by his shell. A piece of paper taped to the wall says it is December 31st. I keep ducking, but nothing is happening. I look around, confused. And then there is a sound effect—crickets. That was my idea.

My classmates laugh, and, standing next to the television cart, I laugh, too. It doesn't feel mean. It feels good. It feels right.

Onscreen, I straighten up and look around. The date on the wall changes to January 1st, but the crickets are still chirping. And, still, nothing is happening. Everyone laughs again, though it's a little quieter this time.

The next shot is me, sitting at Riley's kitchen table. I can see how unsure I was at that moment—my hands are shaking a little, and I keep nervously touching my chin. I hope no one else notices.

"I expected the world to end at the stroke of midnight on January 1st, 2000," I say. I'm reading from my sketchbook, but I'm trying to make eye contact with the camera, too. Inspiration from Trinity, I guess. "But the world didn't end. Everything rolled over correctly. Which is good. But I was incredibly embarrassed, which was not so good."

The screen changes to a painting of a girl on horseback, a flag half hoisted over her shoulder. We found lots of artists' depictions of Joan of Arc—sculptures and paintings and costumes—but this particular painting was by far my favorite. In it, Joan's armor is golden and scalloped and intricate. She's on a big white horse, like a knight from a fairytale. Her face is calm. Ready. Prepared. Her eyes are gazing forward. Even the horse looks excited about the coming battle. I hear the me on the video tape take a deep breath. "Joan of Arc once said, *I am not afraid. I was born to do this.'* And I'm no Joan of Arc, but this quote really struck me. I wasn't afraid of Y2K, not really. What I was afraid of was not being prepared and something terrible and unexpected happening to the people I love."

And then, there's a photo slideshow of my own. Me, much younger, hugging my Mom around the leg. Me and Dad sitting on the sofa, video game controllers in both of our laps. Me holding a cookie out to baby Shelby, trying to entice her to take her first steps. Me, Mom, and Shelby at the beach, pointing excitedly toward our newly constructed sand castle. Dad, Shelby, and me at the aquarium, posing in front of the shark tank. The picture Rich took on Christmas Eve: me, Shelby, and Mom, the three of us huddled in front of the cactus, Mom's arms around Shelby and me like a cocoon. Me standing between a sitting Nana and Pop, my face smooshed between their faces. The screen fades back to me sitting at Riley's table.

"Joan of Arc believed her destiny was to instruct her king on the best way to win a war. I don't know what my destiny is in this millennium. I'm only twelve, and a millennium is a long time. But I know I was born to look at things differently. Some may say that makes me weird. I'm okay with that. My weirdness has allowed me to plan for when things go wrong. And I can use those plans to protect my family and friends. So, I'm going to keep on doing that this millennium, for as long as I can. Because that's what I was born to do. To be a protector."

The video ends with the last few seconds of the black and white cartoon—school children yelling "duck and cover" offscreen, and the turtle scrambling back into his shell. When the screen fades to black, I reach over and push the square button to stop the video. I hear the gears inside the video camera click to a halt.

I wait, quietly, for the same polite applause that Trinity received. But I'm surprised when the response is louder. I see that a few of my classmates are even smiling as they clap. Riley actually puts his fingers in his mouth and whistles, which is pretty bold for him. Mr. Dennis is nodding while applauding, something he didn't do at the end of Trinity's video.

I walk back to my desk and try to keep my face neutral. I can't help the way I feel inside, though; my head and chest feel tingly, but in a good way. Trinity holds up her non-injured hand as I pass, and I give her a high five.

The rest of the presentations go by in a blur. Videos of my classmates sinking a shot during a basketball game or buzzing in first during an academic team meet. There are slightly embarrassing baby and family photos, a couple of songs sung or played on a guitar. Riley's video shows the pinball machine three times, and it beeps and flashes and growls just like it did when I saw it in person.

The bell rings, dismissing us for the day. I slip on my backpack, like everyone else, and head toward the door, but Mr. Dennis calls me over.

"Dani," he says. "Hang back for a minute."

I nod and try to watch calmly as everyone else files out of the room. But inside, I'm a mess. My stomach hurts; my thoughts are going a mile a minute as though my brain is on a hamster wheel. *I'm probably getting detention for messing up the morning show*, I think. *I pretty much admitted it to Ms. Paige. Maybe Mr. Dennis waited a few days for things to settle down before he decided to hand me my official punishment.* My thoughts spiral even more: *If I have detention, I'll have to stay after school. And if I have to stay after school, I'll have to tell Mom to pick me up. And if I tell Mom what I did, I'm going to be in even more trouble.*

Once the classroom is empty, I walk to Mr. Dennis's desk. I'm confused when he smiles at me. "You did a great job with your video, Dani. I'll be honest: I was kind of surprised. It didn't look like you were working too terribly hard on it this week."

His comment initially stings, but then I decide that may be a pretty fair assessment. So, I just nod.

"I know your project is a little personal, but would you mind if we added it to the morning news broadcast? I think it's the best of the bunch."

I adjust my backpack straps on my shoulders. "I don't have detention?" I ask.

Mr. Dennis squints his eyes, confused. "No. Should you have detention?"

I shake my head so hard that hair flies into my eyes. "Good. I mean, no. I don't want detention. And yes, you can show my video. On the morning news. That's fine." I can feel my cheeks getting red. "Is that all?"

Mr. Dennis nods. It sounds like he's chuckling under his breath, too. "Yes, that's it. Have a good weekend, Dani."

"You too!" I say, but don't look at him. I look at my feet instead as I rush out of the classroom. But I smile all the way to the bus ramp.

"And he said it was the best one! He's going to show it on the morning news," I tell Mom and Dad. We're in the food court at the Palm Mall, each of us eating something different. I have Chinese, Dad has pizza, Mom has a chocolate croissant, and Shelby has chicken nuggets.

Mom dabs at her mouth with a napkin. "Dani, that's fantastic! I'm so proud of you."

"Me too," Dad says. "I think you're a chip off the old block. I used to be pretty good at video editing in college."

"Riley edited a lot of it," I say. I pause to take a bite of my egg roll. "I really owe him one."

Mom nods. "Maybe I can whip up some cookies, and you can take them to him next week."

Shelby's eyes get wide. "I want cookies!" she shouts.

"I've got some popsicles at my apartment," Dad tells her. "You can get one when you come over tonight. How does that sound?"

Shelby cheers, crushing one of the chicken nuggets in her fist.

We finish up and decide to stroll past the stores. Dad and I are huddled together talking; Mom is swinging Shelby's hand in front of us. Shelby whines a little when we pass Best Buddy Factory.

"I want a bear," Shelby says.

"No, you have enough toys at home," Mom says.

I expect Shelby to throw a tantrum, but she just says "Okay," in a whiny voice.

Dad and I pass a store display promoting *The Phantom Menace.* They've used strobe lights and paper stars, and a boombox in the corner plays Darth Vader's "Imperial March." There's an extended light saber and a box holding a toy Storm Trooper. There are other figurines in the display, but I don't recognize them. I poke my finger at the glass.

"Who's that?" I ask.

"Anakin Skywalker," Dad says without even pausing. He points at another figurine—a scary red one. "And that's Darth Maul." He drops his hand and sighs. "You guys are so lucky. When I was your age, there weren't any Star Wars toys. If I wanted a light saber, I either had to send away for one or build my own."

Mom and Shelby stop to look at the display as well. Shelby is looking at her reflection, and she pokes her tongue out. Mom catches her shoulder just before she puts her mouth on the glass.

"It's really a great time to be a kid, Dani. To have access to all the things you love," Dad says. He takes one last look at the display and then continues walking. Mom and Shelby trot after him. As I try to catch up, I realize he's right. I can go on the internet and talk to Riley or look up cheats to make my pumpkins grow quicker on *Bounty Crescent*. I can scan my drawings and share them with people all over the world. I can ask Jeeves any question I have and, within seconds, he has an answer. The present can be scary, but it's also really nice—I like having my computer, my Game Grasp, the internet, my instant messenger. And now the future is something I'm excited for, not something I have to dread or prepare for.

"What do you guys want to do this weekend?" Dad asks when I'm walking beside him once again. I guess he's asking Shelby, too, but he's looking at me. "I got everything finished up at work, so we shouldn't have any interruptions. We can do whatever you two want to do. Within reason, of course," he adds.

We pass Queen Teen Boutique, and I immediately start coughing. I have to take several deep breaths before I can respond. "I did think of one thing we could do," I say, my voice hoarse.

"You? Danielle Collier? Coming up with a plan? I'm shocked," Dad jokes, putting his hand over his heart like he's seconds away from fainting.

I roll my eyes—which are still kind of watery from the body spray—but I'm laughing, too. "It's a good plan," I say. "But I'll definitely need your help. Can we stop by the house first? I need to get a few things."

Chapter Eighteen

January 7th, 2000

A Quick Stop at Mom's

The owner of the general store still looks the same. He's wearing his same pixelated straw hat, his same denim overalls. He thanks me for my crops. When I walk out of the general store, the townspeople greet me, red hearts appearing above their heads. I press a button to chat with a small boy who stands on the roadside scratching a white dog behind the ears.

"Thank you for the peaches, Farmer Dani," the speech bubble says above his head. *"They sure are good in Ma's famous cobbler."* I can't help it—I smile.

Then I save my progress and switch off my Game Grasp.

Then I remember something else I want to do.

I turn on my computer and listen as it boots up, the machinery whirring and beeping. As soon as my desktop is visible on my monitor, I head to Settings. A few clicks later, and the Professor Prepared wallpaper is gone, replaced with a generic beach scene. I don't really like it, but that's okay. I'll replace it with something personal at some point—maybe with a photo of me and

Riley. Or maybe not. I don't have to know right now. I can take my time.

There's a soft knock on my door. Dad sticks his head in. He's giving Shelby a piggy back ride, and she's reaching up, touching the top of my door frame with her tiny fingers. "I'm here," Dad says. "Are you ready to head out?"

I nod and quickly shut down my computer. Then I walk over to one of the large cardboard boxes stacked on my floor. "I'm ready," I say, hefting up the heavy box. "But this is where I'm going to need your help."

Dad parks the station wagon in a mostly empty parking lot in front of a long, beige building. There's a sign above the door with a cactus painted on one side and a palm tree on the other: *Oasis Food Bank*, it reads.

We unpack the two heavy, full boxes from the trunk and walk toward the entrance. Shelby skips along behind me, holding the hem of my t-shirt.

Inside, an older woman sits behind a desk. "Can I help you?" she asks.

"I called earlier," Dad says, shifting his box from one arm to the other. "We're here to make a donation."

"Splendid!" the woman says, and claps her wrinkled hands together. "Thank you so much."

Dad shakes his head. "Don't thank me," he says, then inclines his head to where I stand with the other box. "This was all my daughter's idea." Then he looks at the box in his hands. "I lost count of all the cans she loaded up. She's donated some batteries and toiletries, too."

I feel proud when I realize he's right. Inside the boxes are the cans of nonperishable food and containers of water and cleaning supplies and first aid kits that I meticulously gathered and organized on my shelves. I made sure they were intact, dusted them, and checked their expiration dates. They were my harvest. And now they're coming here to do some good in my community, just like the crops that I donate to my townspeople. There's a part of me that feels a little panic at the idea of parting with everything—*what if something happens, and we need this can of black beans? What if the electricity goes out, and we need these flashlights?*—but I try to extinguish those feelings.

The older woman gazes at me behind her bifocals. "Thank you very much, young lady," she says. She types something into a computer on her desk, and for a brief moment, I think about how glad I am that Y2K didn't cause this food bank any problems. "Just follow me, and you can drop your items off and see our warehouse."

The woman stands and opens a big metal door, and Dad, Shelby, and I step into a huge, open space. The floors and walls are bare concrete, but there are countless rows of wooden shelves holding food and diapers and hygiene items. There are people in *volunteer* vests stocking cans on the shelves and unloading boxes. One man in a hard hat operates a forklift, and the loud beeping causes Shelby to huddle closer to my side.

The older woman leads us to a tall man who is clutching a clipboard and scanning the activity all around him.

"These people are here to make a donation," the older woman says. She squeezes my shoulder before she leaves through the metal door, and something about the gesture makes me feel warm all the way to my toes.

The tall man sits his clipboard aside. "Oh yeah," he says, smiling. "We spoke on the phone earlier." He quickly shakes Dad's hand, then he looks toward me. "You must be Dani, right? Your Dad told me a lot about you. I'm Lyle, the Operations Manager here."

I nod and also shake his hand. I can feel the blush on my cheeks. *Dad told him about me?*

Lyle looks over our boxes. "Wow, Dani, thank you. This will feed a few families, at least. You should be very proud of yourself."

"She's amazing," Dad says. I'm surprised, but it's a good kind of surprise.

"I can tell," Lyle says. My face is practically glowing at this point. "You know, your dad was telling me about all these special talents you have. We can always use volunteers who know how to organize and plan and take care of other people." He gestures to where some of the volunteers are currently working. "I'd love to have your help at *Oasis* sometime."

I turn my head to watch the volunteers, their hands working quickly and in sync. Lyle is right; organizing and helping sounds like a perfect fit. "I'd like that, too," I say, a little loudly since it's so noisy in the warehouse.

"We have some rules, though. You'll need to have your Dad volunteer with you until you're fifteen. Maybe it's something you guys can all do together on the weekend." Lyle looks at Shelby. "We even find jobs for the little ones." Shelby is suddenly shy, and she hides her face in my shirt, but Lyle only laughs.

"Sounds like a good weekend to me," Dad says. "What do you think, Dani?"

"Yeah," I say. It sounds more than good—just the thought of working here makes me feel important and needed and not weird at all. Or maybe still weird, but a good type of weird. The type that helps people. I smile and nod, even though I really want to jump up and down and run a lap around the warehouse and give the guy on the forklift a high five. "That sounds really great, actually."

"All right," Lyle says. "I'm going to hold you to that. You can leave your boxes with me."

We sit the heavy boxes down next to Lyle and, this time, the thought of letting it all go doesn't bother me at all.

Back in the parking lot, Dad buckles Shelby into her booster seat. Then we climb in and fasten our own seatbelts. Dad drums his hands against the steering wheel.

"Well," he says, "That didn't take long at all. We've still got the whole evening ahead of us. Anything else you want to do?"

I realize I don't have any sort of plan. And that should scare me, I guess. No plan. No supplies. But, despite that, I feel free, like I could float out of the car like a balloon. It may be the happiest I've felt this millennium.

"Let's just drive," I say. And I smile at Dad as he puts the key in the ignition.

CHAPTER EIGHTEEN

Some Exciting News!

By: Professor Prepared (professorprepared.com)

I have two positive pieces of information to share with all of you today:

1. *We made it past the predicted Leap Day 2K without any major reported problems. I can't help but think this is due in large part to this website and you, my faithful readers, spreading this information and giving computer programmers enough time to ensure their systems were working correctly. Pat yourselves on the back.*

2. *I have written a book! Professor Prepared's Precise Predictions is now available for pre-order. It's chock-full of shocking information about what other catastrophes await us in this millennium—including some scary news about the year 2012 as predicted by the Mayan calendar.*

As always, stay safe, stay informed, and prepare for the worst— by buying my book, of course. Good luck to you!

Need a Professor Prepared bookmark to hold your place in Professor Prepared's Precise Predictions? Click here to visit the Professor Prepared Store!

Teacher and Parent Guide

Use the following questions to guide classroom discussions, book clubs, literature circles, or as simple conversation starters with young readers.

Examining Setting

1. *Doomsday Dani* is set in late 1999. Based on details in the text, compare and contrast how the following technologies worked in 1999 with how they work today:

    a. Telephones

    b. Computers

    c. Internet

    d. Instant Messaging/Texting

    e. Video Recording

2. What does Dani's bedroom tell us about her?

3. Dani lives in Phoenix, Arizona, part of the American Southwest. This area is known for its deserts—dry, barren land with little to no rainfall where only the toughest plants, like cacti— survive. With that in mind, how does the setting

of Phoenix, Arizona and the desert add to the **mood** and **tone** of *Doomsday Dani?*

Examining Characters

1. Characters who change throughout the course of a story are known as **dynamic characters**, while characters that stay the same are known as **flat characters.** How is Dani Collier a dynamic character? Are there any flat characters?

2. How is Trinity the **antagonist** of the story?

3. **Indirect characterization** occurs when one examines a character's thoughts, actions, appearance, and dialogue in order to draw conclusions. In the following scenes, what do readers learn about the character of Dani Collier?

   a. Dani's interaction with her grandparents

   b. Dani's trip to the mall with Riley

   c. Dani's comforting of Shelby in her dad's apartment

   d. Dani's reaction on New Year's Eve

   e. Dani's sabotage of Trinity

Examining Point-of-View

1. *Doomsday Dani* is written in **first person point-of-view.** How might the story be different if it were told in **third person point-of-view?**

Examining Conflict

1. Find examples of the following conflicts in the text:

   a. Man vs. Man

   b. Man vs. Self

   c. Man vs. Nature

   d. Man vs. Society

Examining Speaker Reliability

1. When deciding whether or not a source is reliable, it's important to check the author's credentials—or **authority**—on the topic. Does Professor Prepared have a great deal of authority on the topic of Y2K? What does that tell readers about the reliability of his website?

2. How does Professor Prepared end each blog post? Why is that a red flag?

3. Make a prediction: What would Professor Prepared's website look like in the year 2023?

Acknowledgements

Like Dani Collier, I am a planner. Unlike Dani Collier, I know that I can't do it alone. I am forever grateful to the many people who played a role in bringing my first novel to fruition.

To Arielle Haughee and the team at Orange Blossom Publishing: thank you for taking a chance on my little book, seeing my vision, and answering my many questions. You've truly made a lifelong dream come true, and I'm proud to be part of your team.

I would be remiss not to thank the earliest readers of *Doomsday Dani*, the SENF Writing Group—Joseph, Jake, and Deri. Thank you for your friendship, feedback, and good-natured ribbing when needed. I don't think there would be any *Doomsday Dani* without the three of you. Can we push our meeting to next week?

Thank you to my professors and fellow students at Eastern Kentucky University's Bluegrass Writers Studio. Your MFA program made me a better writer, but also a better reader and teacher.

There are three fantastic schools that are near and dear to my heart: Madison Central High School in Richmond, Kentucky; McKemy Academy of International Studies in Tempe, Arizona; and Francis

ACKNOWLEDGEMENTS

Parker School in Louisville, Kentucky. I have been fortunate to have the unwavering support of my administrators and co-workers throughout the entirety of my teaching—and now writing—career.

To my students, both past and present: never doubt that your dreams are attainable. This book is proof of that. Now, go and write your story. I can't wait to read it.

About the Author

Carissa Turpin was born and raised in Eastern Kentucky, though she lived briefly in Phoenix, Arizona. She currently resides in Louisville, Kentucky, where she teaches fifth and seventh grade Language Arts. She's a dog mom, book hoarder, and proud Y2K survivor. *Doomsday Dani* is her first novel.

More from Orange Blossom Publishing

In the near distant future, Emma's life revolves around the company's Mars terraforming fasttrack program. Stuck between her parents' never-ending Mars shuttle supply runs and her own coursework in the program, Emma dreams of adventure outside of the company's plan for her. Anything to get away from the constant bullying and monotonous coursework.

She finds that adventure accidentally when she stumbles into a portal to a new world. On Merah, she finds two species, the secretive Kabiren, who create and run all technological advancement, and the Amethites, the native species of the planet. When the Kabiren inform her that a portal back to her world does not exist, she accepts a place in their society, as a Protector.

Now she must navigate this assignment of guarding her new planet from portal intruders while also figuring out what the Kabiren are hiding. Her acceptance of her new life without her family and friends is thrown into chaos when she meets a portal intruder: her best friend from Earth. Now she must decide between accepting her adventure in this new world, or fighting for her old one.

The Stone Angel Society is a collection of five short stories about ghosts and the living who believe in them.

Delightfully spooky, these Middle Grade stories provide just the right amount of chills for young readers.

Throughout the book, pages are filled with detailed black and white illustrations to spark young imaginations and make it an even more spooktacular read!

The Stone Angel Society Journal One, the first book in the series, is filled with ghosts found in an old seaside hotel, a haunted house, a children's zoo, a Halloween display and Peaceful Acres Cemetery.

The perfect read for a dark and stormy night, The Stone Angel Society promises to leave the reader open to the very real possibility that we actually might not be alone...

CPSIA information can be obtained
at www.ICGtesting.com
Printed in the USA
BVHW042105090323
660102BV00001B/1